Shannon _____ p, like she'd just drank three espressos. "Well, actually," she said, clicking o___ her Internet browser to launch it, "this all has ___ with BetterLife. My avatar, Sassygirl48 . . ."

I ___ed. "But Maggie said you were having prob___ s at school?"

S___non closed her eyes and nodded. "That ___ust a couple days ago. People whispering ___walked into the room, throwing spitballs at ___ little things. I found out that afternoon ___eone posted footage of Sassygirl48 being ___ uVid."

___t with plenty of bullies in my life, but they ___ways easy to confront. It's hard to yell an ___ someone, or throw something at her, and ___anonymous. On the Internet, though, every-___nonymous. Which makes it incredibly easy ___someone's feelings with no repercussions.

___ed her shoulder. "All right," I said. "You have ___rd that I'm going to find the person who ___ this and make sure it _ends_. Nobody deserves ___eated like this. Nancy Drew is on the case."

NANCY DREW

Available from Aladdin Paperbacks

CAROLYN KEENE

NANCY DREW

GIRL DETECTIVE®

SECRET IDENTITY

#33

**Book One in the
Identity Mystery Trilogy**

Aladdin Paperbacks
New York   London   Toronto   Sydney

This book is a work of fiction. Any references to historical events, real people, or real locales are used fictitiously. Other names, characters, places, and incidents are the product of the author's imagination, and any resemblance to actual events or locales or persons, living or dead, is entirely coincidental.

❧ALADDIN PAPERBACKS
An imprint of Simon & Schuster Children's Publishing Division
1230 Avenue of the Americas, New York, NY 10020
Copyright © 2008 by Simon & Schuster, Inc.
All rights reserved, including the right of
reproduction in whole or in part in any form.
NANCY DREW, NANCY DREW: GIRL DETECTIVE, ALADDIN PAPER-
BACKS, and related logo are registered trademarks of Simon & Schuster, Inc.
Manufactured in the United States of America
First Aladdin Paperbacks edition December 2008
10 9 8 7 6 5 4 3
Library of Congress Control Number 2008920582
ISBN-13: 978-1-4169-6827-6
ISBN-10: 1-4169-6827-X

Contents

SECRET IDENTITY

PROLOGUE

Thank goodness her friend picked up the phone on the first ring. "Hey there."

She felt like she might explode from excitement. "Oh . . . my . . . gosh. You will not believe what is happening to me right now."

Her friend sounded wary. "What?"

"Well, I've been playing BetterLife ever since I got home."

"Duh. That's practically all you do these days."

She couldn't help smiling. That wasn't far from the truth. But the virtual-reality site had become *the* place to be over the last couple months; she probably socialized more online than she did in real life. "Stop. So Sassy Girl Forty-eight is at the mall, and guess who started flirting with me there?"

"Santa Claus."

She sighed. "No. Come on, be serious."

There was a pause of a few seconds. "I don't know. Why don't you tell me?"

"Jake!" she squealed and paused, waiting for the news to sink in. "Jake. Jake Seltzer! Isn't that amazing?"

There was another pause. "But he'd have a different username and look, right? I mean, it's a game, not real life. How did you know it was him?"

She sighed again. "Dude, his character in the game looks just like him. He has the blue streak in his hair, and the nose ring. His name is Guitar Lover Fifteen, and you know how Jake likes music. It has to be him!"

"Wow." Her friend seemed to mull over this information for a few seconds. "The guy you have a crush on is flirting with you online? Do you think he knows who you really are?"

"I think he does. He's said a few things about seeing me in real life, or wanting to flirt with me in real life but being too shy." She smiled to herself. Her heart was beating double-time; that's how excited Jake made her. On-screen, his character was smiling at her adoringly. Other virtual characters walked through the mall all around them, but it was like they were the only two people in the world.

Suddenly there was a loud beep, and she glanced at the dialogue box, where a new message from GuitarLvr15 to Sassygirl48 had appeared.

I LIKE UR BLOND HAIR. U R SO PRETTY, U MUST HAVE GUYS FALLING ALL OVER U.

She squealed. "Oh gosh! You won't believe what he just said." She read the message off to her friend, smiling bigger with each word.

"Wow! Is he talking about you or your avatar?"

She turned to the screen. Her avatar, which she'd spent a week designing, looked as much like her as she'd been able to get: long blond hair, brown eyes, petite. She wore the trendiest clothes she could find; when the outfits available on the site looked too boring, she'd designed her own. All in all, the character was her virtual mini-me. But still . . . "I think he's talking about me. He knows who I am, and he's trying to flirt! We're totally meant to be!"

Her friend let out a breath. "This is almost too good to be true! You should write back, 'You're the only guy I care about.'"

The girl giggled, shaking her head. "Ha! I should, really. Do you think?"

"Totally. I'm being serious."

She gulped. Clicking on the dialogue box, she typed:

U R THE ONLY BOY I CARE ABOUT.

She paused, her mouse hovering over the Send button. Was it time to let Jake know about her crush? She'd hesitated all this time because she didn't want to get hurt. But now it seemed clearer than clear that Jake liked her just as much as she liked him.

Quickly, before she could think better of it, she clicked back into the box and added:

IT'S BEEN THAT WAY FOR A LONG TIME.

She clicked send. "Omigod. You won't believe what I just sent." She read the message back to her friend.

"'Omigosh' is right! Well, now he'll know you like him."

She gulped. "Really like him. But does he like me?"

Beep. She felt her stomach clench as she turned back to the computer for his answer. A new comment had appeared in the dialogue box. She almost felt too nervous to read it, but it drew her eyes like a magnet.

I CARE ABOUT U 2. I'VE JUST BEEN 2 SHY TO TELL U IN REAL
LIFE.

She gasped.

"What's up?"

"He wrote back." She read his message to her friend, feeling like she might float away. Was this really happening? The guy of her dreams, liking her too?

Beep. Another comment popped up on her screen.

MAYBE WE SHOULD GET TOGETHER IN REAL LIFE
SOMETIME.

"Oh wow." She thought her heart might beat out of her chest. "He just wrote more! He wants to get together sometime. In real life."

"Gosh." Her friend didn't sound as excited as she was, but that was to be expected. "That's great, Shannon. I mean, that's really exciting! Are you going to meet him?"

"Duh." She smiled. *Dozens of girls would jump at the chance to date Jake Seltzer,* she thought as she clicked in the dialogue box to respond. *Well, now they'll all be jealous of me.*

Jake's avatar was still smiling at her, waiting for

a response. She made her character nod as she quickly typed, THAT SOUNDS GREAT. JUST TELL ME WHERE AND WHEN. . . .

GuitarLvr15's smile widened. Even in the game, his eyes were bright blue, and they seemed to twinkle extragorgeously as he took Sassygirl48's hand and squeezed it. Her computer beeped again and another message came through.

I KNOW WHO U ARE. I'LL E-MAIL U. WE CAN MAKE PLANS THEN.

"Oh." She couldn't help gasping to her friend, squeezing the phone to her ear. "Oh, he's going to e-mail me! This is so perfect. . . ."

Her friend sounded rushed. "That's great, Shannon. I have to go, though—my mom just called us down for dinner."

"Oh, okay." She felt a little disappointed. She'd wanted to discuss this whole thing until it finally seemed real to her. Still, she couldn't complain. She couldn't stop staring at her computer screen, even though GuitarLvr15 was walking away. "Do you think he'll e-mail me right now? Or will it take a few hours . . . ?"

"I don't know. . . . It sounded like he was going to do it right away."

Shannon smiled. "Okay. I'll tell you what he writes to me."

"Totally. Bye."

"Bye."

She let out a satisfied sigh. It was all so perfect: The guy she'd always known was meant for her actually liked her back. She'd always daydreamed about ending up with Jake, and now it was actually happening.

A little chime sounded as a window popped up on her screen: YOU HAVE NEW MAIL. Her heart quickening, she brought up her account and quickly logged in. *Where should we go on our first date?* she wondered. *Dinner would be great, but what's a romantic restaurant . . . ?*

As the e-mail came up, she scanned the first few lines and felt her heart jump into her throat.

SASSYGIRL48,
DON'T GET YOUR HOPES UP. EVEN IN CYBERSPACE, I WOULD NEVER BE CAUGHT DEAD WITH A STUCK-UP WASTE OF SPACE LIKE YOU.
YOU DESERVE TO BE ALONE—IN THIS GAME, IN REAL LIFE, ALWAYS. YOU DESERVE TO SUFFER LIKE YOU'VE MADE OTHERS SUFFER.

HOME SWEET MYSTERY

"**I**s this the sort of romantic dinner you had in mind?" I couldn't help but smile as my boyfriend Ned took my hand and whispered to me as we moved into his dining room for dinner. We'd been apart for a week, since I'd been on a supercomplicated case that had brought me to New York, and had planned to make tonight our official "catch-up date" at our favorite Italian restaurant. But this afternoon Ned had called with a change in plans: there'd been a mix-up with faculty housing at the university, so he volunteered to host a visiting professor from Iran and his family at the Nickerson home. They wanted to have a small dinner to welcome them, and tonight was the only night that worked for everyone.

I leaned in close to him. "Romance, shromance. A piece of your mother's apple pie will make up for anything we missed."

Ned chuckled and squeezed my hand. "Maybe so. But we'll have to plan a make-up date."

"Agreed." I squeezed back and smiled.

The truth was, it still felt nice to be back in River Heights and doing all the normal things I like to do that don't involve cab chases or setting things on fire. My most recent case had turned into something bigger and crazier than I ever could have anticipated, and I was enjoying being "Normal Nancy" again, instead of "Action Hero Nancy." Being back in Ned's house felt wonderful. And the Nickersons' new houseguests, Professor Mirza al-Fulani and his daughter, Arij, who was twelve, plus his son, Ibrahim, who was sixteen, just couldn't be nicer.

"So, Nancy," Ibrahim began with a smile as we sat down at the dining room table, "have your travels for investigations ever taken you out of the country? Have you been to the Middle East at all?"

I smiled. The al-Fulanis were from Iran, and I was enjoying Ibrahim's upbeat attempts to understand American culture. "I'm afraid not, Ibrahim.

I don't get the chance to travel all that much, even within the United States. But I would love to visit the Middle East someday. There's so much history there."

Professor al-Fulani smiled at me. "This is true, Nancy. It is still sometimes strange for my children and I to wrap our heads around American history, because your country is so new. So much has changed in only two hundred years, whereas in our part of the world, there are thousands of years of history."

Ibrahim piped up excitedly. "Will we study American history at the high school, Nancy?"

I nodded. "Actually, you will, Ibrahim. It's a required class for juniors."

"Excellent." Ibrahim dug into his salad with a grin, glancing at his sister. "I want to learn as much as I can about this country while we are here. I am so eager to meet my classmates."

Arij smiled and nodded, glancing at Ned and me. "Maybe you could look at the outfit I plan to wear tomorrow, Nancy," she said shyly. "I want to fit in well, and make friends quickly."

I laughed. "I don't know if I'm the best person to give fashion advice, but I'd be happy to offer my opinion!"

Ned squeezed my arm. "Don't sell yourself

short, Nance," he cautioned. "After all, you are the reigning Miss Pretty Face River Heights!"

I rolled my eyes at him. While that was true, I wasn't exactly aching to talk about my short and ill-fated career as a pageant queen, which had been part of the case I'd been investigating in New York City. Still, he was smiling. I knew he found my totally out-of-character pageant win amusing.

"Nancy," Ibrahim said, "I am curious about how you solve cases. You have told us a little about your unusual hobby, and I must ask: Do you wear disguises? Do you ever have to lie to people to get the information you need?"

I squirmed in my seat. Ibrahim's face was warm and open, and I knew his questions were coming from an honest curiosity. Still, I liked to keep my trade secrets and didn't exactly want to confess to bending the truth in the service of, well, the truth in front of Ned's father and a bunch of people I'd just met.

"Let's just say I do what the case requires," I replied, reaching for the bread basket. "Every case is different. More bread, anybody?"

Mrs. Nickerson chuckled.

"Ibrahim and Arij," Ned cut in smoothly, "have you ever been to an American high school before, or will tomorrow be your first time?"

"Oh no," Ibrahim replied, shaking his head. "We have attended school in America before. My father travels often for work, you know, and we have traveled with him for months at a time."

Professor al-Fulani nodded. "My children lived with me while I taught at a university in Wisconsin, and also briefly in Florida. Unfortunately both placements were only for a few months, so they weren't able to settle in as much as they would have liked."

Arij nodded, pushing her salad around on her plate. "Sometimes it's hard to make friends," she admitted, a note of sadness creeping into her voice. "People hear my accent or they see my hijab and they think . . . They think I am something that I am not."

Silence bloomed around the table. I nodded sympathetically, imagining how difficult it must be for Arij and Ibrahim to fit in.

"I don't think that will be the case here, Arij," Ned said in a warm voice. "At least, I hope not. We're a university town, and used to diversity."

Mr. Nickerson cleared his throat. "You have any trouble, Arij or Ibrahim, and you let me know," he added. "Ned and I will do everything we can to make your stay here as pleasant as possible."

Arij smiled. She looked a little relieved. "I can't wait to meet everyone," she said quietly.

"Ibrahim and Arij seem very nice," I remarked to Ned a couple hours later as we stood on his porch to say our good nights. "I think they'll enjoy living here, don't you? I think they'll have a good experience at the high school."

Ned nodded. "I hope so," he admitted. "They're definitely a couple of great kids—so friendly and curious. I think as long as their classmates give them a chance, they'll have plenty of friends."

I nodded. The night was growing darker, and crickets chirped in the distance. I took a deep breath. River Heights, I thought happily. Home.

"So . . . ," Ned began, reaching out to squeeze my hand.

"So," I repeated, looking up at him with a smile. "Dinner? Later this week? Just the two of us?"

Ned grinned and nodded. "I'll call you," he said, leaning over to give me a peck on the cheek. "I'm so glad you're back, safe and sound."

"Me too," I said honestly, squeezing his hand again. "Thank your mom for dinner. It was delicious."

Stepping down onto the driveway, I pulled out the keys to my hybrid car and felt a wave of exhaustion wash over me. I imagined my nice warm bed at home, beckoning me. Without a case or anything urgent on the agenda, I could sleep in a bit tomorrow, too. I sighed, carefully driving through the streets that led me home. What a relief to be back among the people I loved, and with a little downtime.

At home, I parked the car in our driveway and yawned as I walked around to the back door. I felt like I had tunnel vision—all I could see was the route to my bedroom, where I'd soon be off to dreamland. Which is why I didn't notice that the kitchen light was on. And three people were sitting at the kitchen table, watching me curiously.

"Nancy?"

A familiar voice pulled me out of my tunnel vision, and I turned to find an unusual sight: my friend Bess; her twelve-year-old sister, Maggie; and our housekeeper and unofficial member of the family, Hannah, were munching on oatmeal-raisin cookies.

"Bess?" I asked, walking in. What on Earth?

Bess stood, placing her hand on Maggie's shoulder. "We were waiting for you to come home," she said. "Hope you're not too tired, Nance. Because I think we've got a case for you."

CYBERVICTIM

"**S**o, this is someone you know from school?" I asked Maggie as she, Bess, and I made the short drive to the house of one Shannon Fitzgerald. Maggie had told me that Shannon was having a lot of trouble at school and had even stayed home that day. Maggie thought I might be able to help.

Maggie nodded. "I've known Shannon since we were in first grade. And now she's in about half my classes."

Hmm. I flipped on my turn signal and pulled onto Shannon's street. "You said she's losing sleep over the problem."

"That's right." Maggie looked like she felt

terrible for her classmate. "She's really having a tough time. I hope you can help her."

"Me too," I agreed, parking in front of the Fitzgeralds' house. "Before we go in, can you tell me anything else? Is this a teacher problem, a problem with bullies . . . ?"

Climbing out of my car, Bess and Maggie exchanged perplexed glances. "It's probably easier to show you in person," Bess explained, touching my shoulder. "Let's put it this way: It's nothing we had to deal with when *we* were in middle school."

Hmm, again. I'd been exhausted just minutes ago, but now the excitement of a new case had woken me up a little. We walked up the neatly tended pathway to the Fitzgeralds' front door, and Maggie rang the doorbell. A few seconds later a confused-looking middle-aged woman opened the door.

"Hello?"

"Hi," Maggie greeted her smoothly. "We're sorry to come over so late. I'm Shannon's friend, Maggie?"

"Oh yes," the woman said slowly, nodding. "Shannon told us you might be coming by with some friends."

"We just need to talk to her for a few minutes," Bess explained.

The woman looked us over curiously, but didn't protest. "Okay," she said, backing into the house. "Shannon's room is upstairs, the second door on the left. Just don't be too long."

"We won't," I promised. I was still hoping to get to bed by a reasonable hour.

The Fitzgeralds' house was large and impressively neat, with wide stairs leading up to an open balcony that led into a warm, brightly lit hallway. Loud emo music played from behind a door decorated with a million sparkly stickers.

Maggie raised her hand to knock.

Before she could make contact, though, the door opened, revealing a pretty blond-haired girl. I knew she was supposed to be in Maggie's grade, but she looked older—at least fourteen. Shannon wore pink shimmery eye shadow; mascara; and shiny, rose-colored lip gloss. Her highlighted blond hair fell down her back in carefully arranged waves. She was, honestly, the most put-together twelve-year-old *I'd* ever seen. I fingered my own messy ponytail with a frown.

"I thought I heard someone," she said quickly, looking us all over with a frantic energy. "Maggie, is this her? Is this your sister's friend Nancy?"

Maggie gestured for Shannon to let us into her room, and Shannon reluctantly stepped aside, never taking her eyes off our faces. Bess and I sat gingerly on the end of a perfectly appointed queen-size bed, and Maggie settled into a desk chair.

"Shannon, this is my sister, Bess, and her friend Nancy Drew," Maggie announced, pointing to us in turn. "I told Nancy you were having a tough time, but I didn't go into details. I figured you could show us."

Shannon nodded quickly. She seemed terribly keyed up, like she'd just drank three espressos. She walked over to a computer that sat on a modern stainless-steel desk and jiggled the mouse. "Well, actually," she said, clicking onto her Internet browser to launch it, "this all has to do with BetterLife. My avatar, Sassygirl48—"

"Wait a minute, wait a minute," I interrupted, walking over to get a better look at the computer monitor. "What did you just say? BetterLife?"

Shannon turned from the screen to face me, her perfectly shaped eyebrows furrowed with confusion. "You don't know what BetterLife is?"

"Remember, Shannon," Maggie piped up apologetically, "they're older."

"Oh." Shannon pursed her lips, not exactly looking thrilled with this development. "Okay. Well. Let's see. BetterLife . . ."

"Isn't it kind of like a virtual-reality thing?" Bess asked, scooting closer to us on the bed. "Like Second Life, where you create a character in a whole virtual world. George told me about it."

"That's right," Maggie confirmed. "You create a character—it can look like you or not—and you give it a name. Basically you play your character, living in this alternate world and interacting with all kinds of other virtual people."

Shannon nodded. "You have your own virtual job and place to live," she added, as the Better-Life home page came up on her browser and she clicked into the user login box. "And there's a special community for River Heights Middle School, where all the kids from school hang out."

I watched as she typed SASSYGIRL48 in the user-ID box, then clicked down to the password box and entered something with eight characters. "Ta da!" she said, her voice sounding a little hollow and sad as the browser loaded a new page featuring a pretty blond character who looked a lot like Shannon, but even older than how the real Shannon looked. The character was tall and Barbie-ish, with perfect proportions, wearing a stylish pink dress and heels.

WELCOME SASSYGIRL48! The screen greeted us.

YOU HAVE $2 REMAINING AND I FRIEND. YOU HAVE 12 MESSAGES.

The picture on the screen then jumped to life. Shannon's character, the blond, sat nursing a cup of coffee in a mall's coffee shop. All around her, teenage characters chatted, shopped, or just wandered alone. A scroll at the bottom of the page showed Sassygirl48's stats:

HUNGER LEVEL: 8
FRIENDS: 1
JOB: SALON JANITOR
STYLE LEVEL: 7
HAPPINESS: 5

"I don't get it," I blurted.

Shannon looked surprised. "What's not to get?" she asked, leaning over to click on a button that read Messages. "This is my virtual life. Some people go to a coffee shop or a club to socialize, but most kids from my class come on here."

"So to socialize, you sit alone in your room and type on a computer?" I asked, frowning at the screen.

"Not really *alone*," Shannon insisted. "I'm with my friends, just in a different way. There are no limits in a virtual world. We can do anything—

have our own apartments, throw parties, go shop-ping . . ."

"And why not just go shopping?" I asked. "You know, here? In River Heights?"

Maggie and Shannon just stared at me.

"It's okay, Nance," Bess comforted me, stand-ing up and walking over to pat my back. "I didn't get it either."

"Anyway," said Shannon, clicking the mouse and causing a new window to come up. "Come take a look at this. I think this will help explain why I've been so freaked out the last few days."

I looked over Shannon's shoulder at the screen, where a new page was loading.

MESSAGES, it finally read. An assortment of short personal notes was arranged below the headline, like on a message board.

SASSYGIRL48, read the first one. UR A LIAR N A JERK. WHEN I'M FINISHED NO ONE WILL DARE BE FRIENDS W/U. U DESERVE 2 SUFFER.

I gasped. Who would write something so awful?

It was signed at the bottom: GUITARLVR15.

"Oh my gosh," I said breathlessly.

"There's more," Shannon said simply. "Did you read them all?"

I hadn't. I quickly scanned down the remain-ing messages.

I USED 2 THINK U WERE NICE. NOW I KNOW UR A WASTE
OF SPACE. GET OFF BETTERLIFE. ROZ84

I CAN'T BELIEVE U ACT THE WAY U DO N EXPECT PEOPLE
TO LIKE U. PEOPLE LIKE U R ALWAYS ALONE. BUTTERFLY-
DUST

DID U LIKE THE NOTE I LEFT ON UR HOUSE? I'M LEAVING
1 JUST LIKE IT ON UR LOCKER 2MROW. KILLERJOE4

"What's the note he's talking about?" I asked.
"On your house? On your locker?"

Shannon swallowed, shaking her head sadly. She
clicked on a tiny icon at the bottom of the page,
and soon the screen was filled with the image of
a cute, tidy, brick townhouse in a well-landscaped
development. One jarring detail kept the house
from looking inviting: Someone had spray painted
loser with red paint across the front door.

"Oh my gosh," I repeated.

"Yeah." Shannon nodded ruefully. "And yesterday I found the same word written on my locker
in red marker."

My mouth had dropped open. Weren't computer games supposed to be fun? "Who are these
people?" I asked as Shannon clicked back to the
messages page. "Roz Eighty-four? Butterfly Dust?

Killer Joe Four? Are these people you know?"

"Could be." Shannon shrugged, still looking sad. "Or they could be total strangers. I had never heard of any of them before last week."

I frowned. "Did something happen last week?"

Shannon sighed and closed her eyes, nodding. "Yeah. But I didn't expect it to lead to this."

"What happened?" I asked, glancing back at the screen. The cruel messages seemed to go on forever. Words like *nasty, horrible,* and *stupid* jumped out at me, like little daggers.

Shannon swallowed again. She opened her eyes, and when she spoke, it seemed as if she was trying to divorce herself from what she was saying—like if she thought too hard about it, she might cry.

"There's this boy I kind of like in town. He's older than me; sixteen. We haven't talked much in real life, except when I sometimes go to the coffee shop he works at, and we've had, like, little conversations."

I nodded. "Okay."

"I never thought much about it. I figured he was older, so he'd never be interested in a girl my age. But then one afternoon, I'm playing Better-Life and I come across this character who looks *exactly* like my crush."

I glanced at Bess. She looked just as confused by all this as I was. "Right."

Shannon sighed. "We were at the mall—I mean, the *virtual* mall—and he just came up to me and offered me a sip of his smoothie."

I tried to make sense of that. "A *virtual* sip of his . . . *virtual* smoothie."

Shannon shrugged. "Right. It was strawberry. I took a sip, and then he started talking to me—asking me about myself, where I lived, what I was doing at the mall. And then he started"—she bit her lip—"giving me all these *compliments*."

I nodded. "*Virtual* compliments."

Shannon nodded. "At first, yes. He said he liked my hairstyle, liked my dress. But at some point—I forget what was the first thing he actually said—but I started to realize that he was complimenting *me* me, and not me, Sassygirl48."

I nodded slowly. "Riiiiiight."

She sighed. "I know, it sounds crazy. But he started saying things that you wouldn't know from meeting my character in BetterLife. Like that I play the violin, or that I was voted Class Favorite at school last year. And then he said . . ." She paused, frowning.

"He said . . . ?" I prompted.

She sighed again. "He said he'd seen me

around—by then I was sure he meant in real life—but he'd always been too shy to talk to me."

I frowned. "And this boy is sixteen?"

Shannon shook her head. "I know, I know. It seems crazy now. Why would he use a game to flirt with me? But at the time it just made so much, I dunno, *sense*."

I nodded. I was sure it didn't hurt that the boy was telling Shannon exactly what she wanted to hear. "Then what happened?"

Shannon's face fell. "Then we said we would get together sometime in real life. After that, he took off. And his e-mail came."

I glanced at the screen, having an idea where this was going. "And his e-mail said . . . ?"

Shannon sighed, moving toward the computer and typing an address into her browser. Soon the middle-school's web-based e-mail program popped up. "See for yourself."

I leaned in closer to the screen as the message loaded. Then, there it was:

To: SFITZGERALD@RHMS.GRADE6.EDU
FROM: GUITARZRCOOL@FASTMAIL.NET
SASSYGIRL48,
DON'T GET YOUR HOPES UP. EVEN IN CYBERSPACE,

I WOULD NEVER BE CAUGHT DEAD WITH A STUCK-UP
WASTE OF SPACE LIKE YOU.
YOU DESERVE TO BE ALONE—IN THIS GAME, IN REAL
LIFE, ALWAYS. YOU DESERVE TO SUFFER LIKE YOU'VE
MADE OTHERS SUFFER.

I gasped.

Bess was right behind me, reading over my shoulder. "Have you talked to the guy?" she asked, frowning at the e-mail's nasty tone. "Have you asked him why he's so angry at you? Or whether it was really him at all?"

Shannon shrugged, looking down into her lap. For the first time since I'd met her, she'd lost her mature sheen. She looked like a sad, freaked-out twelve-year-old kid. "I'm too embarrassed," she said softly.

"Embarrassed about what?" asked Bess. I could tell she was pretty upset that somebody would target someone Maggie's age through the Internet. "You didn't do anything wrong. You don't deserve to be treated like this!"

Shannon kept staring at her lap, and I placed my hand on her shoulder. "It's okay," I said. "It can be hard to confront a bully. Even if you know you don't deserve to be treated like that."

Shannon nodded and sighed. Bess seemed to

soften, and patted her arm. "I'm sorry. It just really upsets me that this happened to you."

Maggie stood up and walked over to the three of us, asking gently, "Do you want to tell them how it's gone since then, Shannon?"

Shannon nodded. "Yeah," she agreed. "Basically, it's gotten worse and worse. The day after I got that e-mail from GuitarLvr15, I got two more e-mails—from people I'd never heard of. They were just like the messages you see there— I'm terrible, mean, whatever."

I nodded. "Wow."

"Yeah." She frowned. "Little by little, people started being meaner to me in the game. They'd yell things when I walked by, or avoid me when I went to hang out and socialize. At first, it was just a few people, but little by little, it seemed like *everyone* got involved. Even people I'd hung out with in the game before—they didn't want anything to do with me." She paused before continuing. "I work at a salon in the game. I mean, Sassygirl48 does. That's how she pays the bills. But a few days ago I went to work, and my boss suddenly just fired me. She said it was for 'conduct reasons,' but she wouldn't give me any details. I walked home, and all the way, people were yelling things at me on the street. A girl I'd never seen before was eating in the park, and she threw her trash at me. When I got home, and . . . You saw what was painted on the house."

I sighed. "I did. But you said . . . Maggie said you were having problems at school?"

Shannon closed her eyes and nodded. "That started just a couple days ago. People whispering when I walked into the room, throwing spitballs at me, mean little things." She sighed. "I found out that afternoon that someone posted footage of Sassygirl48 being bullied on uVid."

I immediately looked to Bess for an explanation, but she had already turned to Maggie for the same reason.

"It's another website owned by the creators of BetterLife," Maggie explained. "It's sort of a greatest-hits type thing. When you're playing the game, it automatically records your game play every fifteen minutes, so if anything really cool happens, you can save it as a video file and post it to uVid so everyone can watch."

I frowned. "You can just post it anonymously? So no one has any privacy, even in this virtual world?"

Shannon shook her head. "No, you have to post it under your username. But it's no one I know. Just another random stranger who hates me on the Internet." Her voice caught, and she looked into her lap again.

I reached out and touched her shoulder. "I'm sorry to make you relive all this, Shannon, but just so I'm clear: You were being bullied online, and then someone made public a video of your bullying, and now you're being bullied at school?"

Shannon started to cry. I glanced at Maggie, and she nodded. "That's pretty much it," she confirmed.

"Well," I murmured, glancing at Bess. She looked as dismayed by all this as I felt.

I'd dealt with plenty of bullies in my life, but they were always easy to confront, because bullying is such a deliberate act. It's hard to yell an insult at someone, or throw something at her, and remain anonymous. On the Internet, though, everyone is anonymous. Which makes it incredibly easy to hurt someone's feelings with no repercussions.

"It sounds like this first boy, GuitarLvr15, is the ringleader. He threw the first stone, so to speak, and he's still involved, right?" I asked Shannon gently.

She sniffled and nodded. "Right. I keep getting e-mails from him."

I sighed. "Shannon," I said delicately, "is there

any reason this boy would want to hurt you? Have you had any interactions in person, or any interactions with his friends?"

Shannon shook her head vigorously. "That's what's so crazy!" she explained. "I'd never had a real conversation with him until that time in the game. And I was so happy!" She let out a sob.

I patted her shoulder. "All right," I said. "Shannon, I wish I could have kept this from happening to you, but it's too late. You have my word, though, that I'm going to find the person who started this and make sure it *ends*. Nobody deserves to be treated like this."

Shannon looked up at me, blinking away tears. "Thank you, Nancy!" she cried. "When Maggie told me about you, I wasn't sure . . . I didn't know if I trusted someone I didn't know with what was happening to me. But you're so nice! I believe you can stop this."

"Believe it," I agreed, reaching for Shannon's hand and squeezing it. "Nancy Drew is on the case."

Maggie, Bess, and I were silent as I drove them back to my house, since they'd left Bess's car there. We all had pensive expressions, each thinking our own separate thoughts.

"The Internet has made so many things easier,"

I murmured finally. "Including being a bully."

Bess sighed. "It scares me that this whole virtual world has been going on for years now, and I just realized today that Maggie has an account. If someone bullied her online, who knows whether me or my parents would even find out."

Maggie rolled her eyes. "Bess," she chided, "don't be such a worrywart. Of course I'd tell you."

I glanced at Maggie in the rearview mirror. "What's Shannon like at school?" I asked. The truth was, I was having trouble picturing her. It was hard to reconcile the pretty, outgoing girl I'd met with the quieter, more vulnerable kids I remembered being bullied when I was in school. Unless she was completely different around kids her own age.

Maggie smiled. "She's great! She has great style, and she dresses like a celebrity or something, and she always had tons of friends. . . . She used to eat lunch with, like, fifteen people, and it was always hard to get a seat at their table. . . ."

Hmmmm. "So she was pretty popular before the bullying started."

Maggie looked at me like that was obvious. "Yeah. I would say, like, the most popular—one of the most popular girls in our grade."

Verrry interesting. "Does she have any ene-mies?"

Maggie seemed to consider this for a minute, then shook her head. "Shannon isn't any meaner than anyone else. I mean, she's popular, but I think people like her. I don't think she's ever, like, ruined anybody's life or anything."

I nodded slowly, pulling into our driveway. Careful to leave space for Bess to pull out, I parked and turned off the car's engine. "Home again, home again," I sang lightly.

Bess moaned and sat up in the passenger seat. "Speak for yourself," she retorted, opening her door. "Come on, kiddo. I've got a date with my bed that I'm not going to miss for anything." She looked back at me. "Thanks, Nancy. You're a life-saver. I mean it."

I smiled. "Thanks for pointing me in the direc-tion of someone who needs me."

VIRTUAL LIVES

As I showered and dressed the next morning, I had to admit to myself that I was having a little trouble wrapping my head around the whole BetterLife idea. I'd e-mailed Bess and George before bed—I wasn't *hopelessly* computer illiterate—to arrange a time that afternoon for them to come over to help set up a BetterLife identity for me. But for now, I figured, better to stick to the basics of sleuthing: getting out there and asking some questions, person to person.

Barbara's Beans was a cute little coffee shop in downtown River Heights that was popular with the middle-school and high-school crowds.

Situated in an old mill, the shop was huge and airy, with red brick walls that had been covered by murals painted by two decades' worth of River Heights High School art students. A bank of computers was tucked into the right wall, just inside the doors, and they were always filled with kids e-mailing, IMing, or even occasionally—Gasp!—doing homework. Today, though, there was only one kid I was interested in—and he was *behind* the counter.

I scanned the menu. "I'll take a medium—I mean, um, a doppio . . . I mean, a cappuccino with, um, caramel and cinnamon flavoring—"

My target smiled at me. Honestly, he looked a little intimidating, with a ring in his nose and a cobalt blue streak dyed into his shaggy, angular haircut. Up close, his eyes had a warm twinkle that I was sure had influenced Shannon's crush on him. "Milk?"

I nodded. "Yes, please."

He chuckled. "No, I mean what kind of milk would you like. Whole, skim, two percent, soy—"

"*Not* soy," I interrupted him. A few months before, Bess had tried to get George and I on the soy milk bandwagon, as she'd called it, with disastrous results. "Um, whole milk is fine, thanks."

He smiled and nodded. "Decaf? Half caf?"

I nodded. "Caffeinated."

He punched a few numbers into the register. "Don't take this the wrong way," he said with in a just-between-us tone, "but I get the sense you're a bit of a coffee novice."

I'm sure my face fell. "Is it that obvious?"

He smiled. "Did you know that a doppio means a double—two shots of espresso?"

I shook my head. "No! Just one is fine, thanks." I drank coffee maybe a couple times a week. Two shots of espresso and they'd be peeling me off the ceiling.

He nodded. "That'll be three fifty, please."

I handed over the money, glancing up at him out of the corner of my eye. "I have a confession to make," I said. "I'm not just here for the coffee."

He didn't look all that surprised. "No? The computers are right over there," he replied, gesturing.

I shook my head. "No, I mean, I need to ask you some questions."

He looked surprised. "About what?"

"A young girl who's being bullied online," I said slowly, pausing to gauge his reaction. "You wouldn't know anything about that?"

Perhaps this barista was a part-time actor, but I had to admit that he honestly looked stunned by my question, and more than a little lost. "No." He frowned, shaking his head as though to clear it, and placed my money in the cash register, then closed the drawer. "Let me just get someone to cover for me. *Kylie!* Give me a minute, then I'll meet you at that table over there." He pointed at a small table tucked into a private corner surrounded by plants.

I sat down where he told me to, and a minute or two later, a redheaded girl came out from the back and took Jake's place at the counter. I could hear the whirring and gurgling of the espresso machine, and after another minute or so, Jake appeared at the table, holding a foamy cappuccino in a wide, red coffee cup. "Here you go," he said, placing the drink in front of me. "I'm Jake, by the way."

I nodded in greeting. "I'm Nancy."

He settled into the seat across from me. "Now, what were you saying? Something about a girl being bullied?"

I decided to start at the beginning. "Are you familiar with the game BetterLife?"

Jake snorted. It surprised me, and I cast him an annoyed glance over my cappuccino.

"I'm sorry," he said. "It's just . . . that's like asking, 'Have you heard of this restaurant called McDonald's?' I thought everyone had heard of BetterLife."

I stiffened, sipping my drink. "I hadn't," I corrected him. "At least, not until last night. But anyway—"

"Here." Jake suddenly reached out with a napkin and swiped at the tip of my nose. "You had foam. Sorry. Now what about BetterLife?"

I paused, feeling a little silly. Here I was, someone who'd never heard of what was apparently the most popular computer game of all time, and I couldn't even seem to drink a cappuccino properly. Still, I needed to get to the bottom of what Jake knew. "Do you have a character on BetterLife?"

Jake nodded. "Sure."

I sighed. Jake seemed like a nice enough kid, but now I braced myself for the inevitable. "So why have you been attacking Shannon online? She insists she never did anything bad to you, but tell me your side of the story."

But Jake looked confused again. "Who?" he asked. "I'm sorry. Just who do you think I am?"

I frowned. "I think you're Jake Seltzer," I replied. "Here in River Heights. But in the world of BetterLife, I think you go by GuitarLvr15."

I waited for a flash of recognition to pass behind Jake's eyes, but he still looked confused. "Who?" he asked, shaking his head. "Listen, Nancy, I think you have the wrong guy. I'm not sure why you think I'm this Guitar Lover kid. . . ."

"Because he looks *just like you*," I replied, starting to feel a little frustrated. "And he's the ringleader of an angry mob that's targeting a young girl online. You just said you have a BetterLife avatar?"

"Sure." Jake nodded, and started to stand up from his seat. "Hey, why don't we go over to the computers? I can show you my BetterLife character, and maybe you'll believe me when I say I have no idea who this Guitar Lover is."

"Okay," I said hesitantly. I was beginning to feel really confused. If Jake really wasn't Guitar-Lvr15, did that mean someone had purposefully designed the character to look like him? Either to throw Shannon off track, or make her feel like a bigger fool because she'd been humiliated by her crush?

Over at the computers, Jake settled down in front of the huge monitor of a Mac and pulled over a chair for me. "Okay," he said, clicking on the Internet browser icon and briskly typing in the BetterLife URL. It took a few minutes to load, but then the same welcome screen I remembered from last night popped up, an aerial view of a virtual town with a login box on the right. I watched as Jake typed in "BionicEd" and a password, which I read as *bobdylan*. A new page loaded, and slowly we focused in on a tall, thin, somewhat nerdy-looking young man in a scientist's lab coat and thick, black-framed glasses. He sat in a small bedroom with two sets of bunk beds that resembled the dorm rooms at River Heights University.

"This is Bionic Ed," Jake said. "He's a chemistry major at BetterLife University. He loves noodling around with chemicals and someday, he's going to invent an alternative to plastic that's just as durable but totally biodegradable."

I nodded. On-screen, BionicEd stood up from his desk and exited the room. "Is that your dream?" I asked.

Jake frowned. "No," he replied, as if I'd just suggested he dreamed of being the world's first nose-ringed opera singer. "It's BionicEd's dream."

By now, BionicEd was crossing a sunny, well-manicured courtyard that looked similar to, if not exactly like, a courtyard at River Heights University. "This doesn't even look like the same world as the game Shannon was playing," I observed. Where was the idyllic suburban town, the virtual mall, the townhouse?

"That's because it's probably not," Jake replied. A raven-haired beauty wearing surgical scrubs with stiletto heels paused near BionicEd. "There are tons of different forums on BetterLife. They're all completely separate; like their own little worlds. Once you have a character in one, you can move between different forums, but most people don't. I don't hang out in the middle-school or the high-school forum. People are too immature there. BionicEd really belongs in a university setting."

I stared at the screen. "This is the university forum?"

Jake nodded. "RHU, baby!" He'd been typing furiously to "talk" to the dark-haired girl:

HI, HEY WHAZZUP. NUTHIN MUCH, JUST STUDYING; I MISSED U.

Suddenly the girl leaned forward and planted one on BionicEd, right on the lips. BionicEd responded with enthusiasm, and suddenly I felt myself blushing, not quite sure what to do when two virtual characters were virtually making out in their virtual world right in front of you.

"Um . . . Is she your girlfriend?" I asked.

Jake nodded as the characters finally came up for air. "Her name is Doctor Lovely. She's pre-med. We're always together."

I glanced at Jake out of the corner of my eye, taking mental stock. "You're how old? Sixteen?"

Jake nodded. He was typing again. U LOOK ESP LOVELY 2DAY.

I cleared my throat, feeling like a huge fuddy-duddy. "Aren't you a little young to be dating a college student?"

Jake finally looked up from the computer then, looking at me with what seemed like pity. "*I'm* not dating her," he corrected me. "BionicEd is."

"Oh." I looked at the floor, wondering how I'd possibly missed all this stuff. "But in real life, you're just friends."

Jake shrugged, turning back to the computer. "I've never met DoctorLovely before in my life," he replied. "I don't even know who she is, really. She could be a middle-aged father of six for all I know. But in the BetterLife world, she and BionicEd have a thing going on."

I sighed. This was all really going over my head, and I wasn't making any headway on Shannon's case. "So in BetterLife, you don't have to show any proof that you are who you say you are?"

Jake shook his head. "Nope. Why?"

"I mean . . ." I paused, biting my lip. "I could sign up for, say, a community for people retired from the circus, and nobody would ever check that I really was in the circus?"

Jake glanced up, frowning. "That's right," he said, turning back to type more to DoctorLovely. "Although I don't think that community exists."

I sighed again. "And nobody has a problem with that?" I asked.

Jake sighed, glancing from me to the computer screen. He quickly typed GTG to DoctorLovely, then clicked the mouse on to the computer's sleep mode. The screen went from full color to black, and while BionicEd probably continued to move—kind of wandering around the courtyard now, aimless—it was clear that Jake was no longer controlling him. "Why would anyone have a problem with it?" Jake asked me.

"It just seems a little misleading," I replied. "If I sign up for the middle-school community, other users would probably assume I'm in middle school. And besides, if the game is completely anonymous, it means no one is responsible for their own actions."

Jake nodded. "And if I sign up for the university community, and I get along fine with everyone and everyone's fine with that, and it never goes beyond the computer screen . . . So what?"

"The problem is when it goes *beyond* the computer screen. Like the situation I came to talk with you about. A young girl is being harassed in the middle-school forum, and it's gotten so out of control that now people are bullying her in real life."

Jake nodded again. "Like what kind of stuff?"

I glanced at the computer screen. "It would actually be easier to show you." Sitting down in front of the computer, I glanced at my watch. Shannon had given me her username and password last night as well as permission to go into her e-mail if need be, and she had promised me she'd go to school today, meaning she couldn't be playing BetterLife right now. After I woke up the computer, I clicked on a button that said Log Out and was brought back to the initial login screen. Quickly I typed in SASSYGIRL48 and Shannon's password, GLITTERY, and was brought to a screen where Shannon's character sat sadly in a small bedroom.

"She must be home," I murmured. "How do I get her to leave the house?"

"Here." Jake took the mouse from me and with a series of clicks, navigated Sassygirl48 out of her house and onto her lawn.

"Now turn around," I said, and Jake clicked a compass that changed the view on the monitor to the exterior of Sassygirl48's townhouse.

"Wow," he murmured.

The grafitti I'd seen the night before, *loser*, was still spray painted across the house, and now two front windows were broken, as if someone had thrown rocks through them. Sassygirl48's cute house was quickly turning into a dump.

"What's that in the mailbox?" I asked, pointing to a bright white envelope. Jake clicked on it, and the letter appeared on-screen.

DEAR SASSYGIRL48,

YOU HAVE ALWAYS BEEN A GOOD TENANT, BUT RECENTLY, THE NOISE AND NASTY ELEMENT YOU HAVE BROUGHT TO THE DEVELOPMENT ARE SIMPLY TOO MUCH FOR YOUR NEIGHBORS AND ME TO BEAR. I MUST ASK YOU TO VACATE THE PROPERTY BY FRIDAY. IF YOU DO NOT, I WILL PLACE YOUR BELONGINGS ON THE FRONT LAWN AND CHANGE THE LOCKS. I HOPE YOU WILL TAKE THIS ACTION AS ENCOURAGEMENT TO RECONSIDER THE COMPANY YOU KEEP.

SINCERELY,

YOUR LANDLORD

HAMSTERMAN03

"Hamster Man?" I asked.

"It's another player," Jake explained. "When you get wealthy enough in the game, you can buy property and rent to tenants."

"Just like in real life."

"Just like in real life," Jake echoed. "And just like in real life, landlords can evict you."

I shook my head. "Wow." On-screen, noises seemed to be coming from the street—shouts and angry growls. Suddenly a tiny white ball hurled through the air and attached itself to Sassygirl48's shoulder.

"Spitballs," said Jake. He clicked a button, and Sassygirl48 turned to face two girls, one had long, lustrous red hair, sparkling green eyes, and—

"Is that a cow?" I asked.

"Yeah." Jake nodded. "In BetterLife, you can have any pet you want. You can domesticate any animal."

I nodded. The other girl had long, black hair and elaborate, catlike eye makeup. A purple tattoo—a Celtic knot— stood out on her arm.

Beep!

Suddenly a message appeared on-screen.

A MESSAGE FROM ILOVEDUBLIN:
U WASTE OF SPACE, WHY DID U COME TO SCHOOL 2DAY?
EVERYONE IN COMPUTER LAB THINKS U SHOULD GO HOME.

"Whoa," Jake murmured.

Beep. Another one appeared.

A MESSAGE FROM MOOMOOGIRL:
YEAH, NO1 LIKES UR FACE OR UR ATTITUDE. STAY HOME
AND CRY INTO UR CORNFLAKES, LOSER.

"I think I've seen enough," Jake murmured, moving the arrow over to the Logout button.

"Wait," I cautioned, grabbing his arm. "Can you look up another user in the middle-school community?"

Jake frowned. "Kind of," he replied. "If Sassygirl48 has dealt with GuitarLvr15 before, I can call up an image of their last interaction."

I nodded. "That works. I want you to look up GuitarLvr15."

Jake looked doubtful, but clicked on a Search History icon and entered the username. Instantly, a short video popped up of a character that looked like Jake's twin—right down to the black concert T-shirt, nose ring, and blue streak in his hair—shoving Sassygirl48 at the mall.

"That was just yesterday," I said, reading the time stamp on the screen.

"Wow," Jake muttered, squinting at the screen. "*Wow.* That really could be me."

"Yeah," I agreed. "And you're sure you have nothing to do with it?"

Jake shook his head. "It's not me," he replied. "But if you figure out who it is, let me know. They're totally stealing my look."

The video came to an end, and Jake glanced up at me sadly before clicking the Log Out button. "Poor girl," he murmured. "That has to be hard."

"And you're sure you don't know Shannon Fitzgerald?" I asked.

Jake's face totally changed. He went from sadness and pity to shock and amazement, all in a couple seconds. "That's *Shannon Fitzgerald*?" he asked, his mouth dropping open. "Whoa. Yeah, I guess it did kind of look like her."

"Why are you so surprised?" I asked. "Look, whoever this Guitar Lover person is, he flirted with Shannon online before completely turning on her and ringleading a mob of bullies."

"And you thought . . . Oh wow." Jake shook his head. "She thought it was me flirting with her. And then me bullying her."

I nodded. "Can you blame her?"

He shrugged. "It looks just like me," he agreed. "And a lot of kids in the middle school . . . They create avatars that look just like them. Them, in computer form."

"Right." I sighed. "But you didn't."

Jake looked up at me, sympathetic now. "Why go through all the trouble of creating a new character who looks and acts just like you?" he asked. "The game is for fun, for you to try something different. Isn't that the whole point of playing? Not to lead *your* life, but a *better* life?" He sighed. "Besides. Even if that character was me, there's no way I would ever flirt with Shannon Fitzgerald."

My ears perked up. "No? Why?"

Jake made a face. "Let's just say, I've heard she has a mean streak."

Hmm. "What do you mean?"

"She's superpopular, and she loves making fun of the less popular kids. Just last week, I heard she tripped some poor girl in the cafeteria, in front of everyone, supposedly because their English teacher had chosen to read this girl's essay out loud. Shannon called her a teacher's pet. Some kids were talking about it while I was working."

My eyes widened. *This* was interesting. Could this person have turned the bullying around on Shannon and retreated online to do it?

"What's this girl's name?"

"Sarah O'Malley." Jake frowned, standing up

from the computer. "Sheesh. I guess no one really deserves to be harassed online, but if you're Shannon Fitzgerald. . ." He paused. "Maybe it's time she saw what life's like for the other half."

CYBERSLEUTHING

A few hours later, Bess and I flanked George as the three of us sat down in front of my computer.

"Okay, so we're going to create Nancy a BetterLife character, so she can be right in the middle of things. Before we begin," George said, wiggling her fingers in what I guessed were pre-typing and clicking exercises. "You guys *really* had never heard of BetterLife before this? *Really?* For real? I've been on it for months."

I wrinkled my nose indignantly. "For real," I confirmed. "Why? Is it all over the evening news or something?"

"I've been too busy working and keeping up

with fashion trends to waste time on the Internet," Bess retorted with a sniff, reaching over to tug a piece of George's faded blue T-shirt. "Unlike *some* people."

George shook her off, shaking her head. "Okay, okay," she said, firing up my Internet browser. "I just find it a little strange that my two very smart best friends have somehow missed out on this phenomenon, which was on the cover of *Time* magazine last week. . . ."

"It was?" I asked. Wow. I'd thought this was just something teenagers liked.

George nodded, typing the URL for Better-Life into the browser's search field. "It's available free on the Internet, but the creators have been making a ton of money through advertising. And next month they're introducing a subscription service that will allow users access to special features—wardrobe and career upgrades, special talents for your character, making it easier to make videos; that kind of thing. They're expected to make *billions*."

"Huh," I murmured as the login screen loaded. "Will you still be able to play the current version for free?"

"Yeah." George frowned at the login screen, then clicked a button right below the password box: Create User. "But trust me, the upgrades sound awesome enough that nobody will want to be caught dead on the free version."

A new screen popped up, with BUILD YOUR AVATAR! written across the top. A somewhat bland-looking blond guy stood in the middle of the screen, with arrows on either side of his hair, face, body, and shoes. George clicked on a button marked Gender, and selected Female. The blond guy turned into a cute blond lady. Then George clicked on a box marked Age, and selected 11–15, glancing sideways at me. "Since we're going to put you in the middle-school community," she explained.

"Fine with me," I agreed. On-screen, the lady became a fresh-faced teenager.

Then George started clicking on the arrows that surrounded the character. After about fifteen minutes, we'd created a cute girl with a strawberry-blond ponytail and blue eyes, clad in a white T-shirt, blue cardigan, and tweed pants with sneakers. "Nancy style," Bess said approvingly. Once we'd selected her appearance, a new screen charged us with naming our character's hobbies and interests.

"How about dancing?" George asked.

"And shopping," Bess added.

I cast them a skeptical glance. The last time I'd gone shopping, a different president had been in office.

George shrugged, typing the hobbies into the correct fields on-screen. "You can't just say sleuthing, Nance," she chided.

"Yeah," Bess piped in. "Suspicious much?"

Finally we were brought to a screen that asked us to name our new character.

"How about Twinkletoes14?" Bess asked.

"Or why don't you just call me Wheresthe-Mall?" I joked.

George shook her head, smiling. "Let's try something simpler," she suggested. Clicking in the box, she typed "VirtualNancy" and clicked the Submit button.

A happy chime sounded, and when the screen reloaded, it proclaimed:

CONGRATULATIONS! YOU HAVE CREATED VIRTUALNANCY. AFTER YOU CLICK ACCEPT, YOUR CHARACTER WILL BE DROPPED INTO THE TOWN'S CENTER WITH $500. WE SUGGEST THAT SHE IMMEDIATELY FIND A JOB AND AN AFFORDABLE PLACE TO LIVE. ONCE SHE HAS THESE TWO THINGS, START EXPLORING! REMEMBER, BETTERLIFE IS JUST LIKE REAL LIFE, BUT BETTER—ANYTHING IS POSSIBLE!

"All right, guys," George announced, clicking the Accept button. "Here goes nothing."

VirtualNancy was dropped into the middle of a virtual town center that looked a little, but not exactly, like River Heights. George explained that in the game, your character could, by buying a newspaper, find jobs but only the ones for which she was "qualified" would pop up—and since VirtualNancy was a newbie, that wouldn't be many. Within a few minutes VirtualNancy had checked out the paper and secured an unglamorous job sweeping up in a hair salon. A trip to the virtual real estate office placed her in a drafty studio apartment on the edge of town—the only place poor VirtualNancy could afford.

"I feel so bad for her," Bess murmured as VirtualNancy huddled under a dirty quilt to stay warm. "Virtual Nancy shouldn't have to live like this!"

George shook her head. "It's all part of the game, Bess," she assured her cousin. "Everyone starts out in humble circumstances. You work your way up."

Sure enough, after just a few days of work (a day in BetterLife seemed to go by in about half an hour), VirtualNancy had earned enough to buy a clean comforter and some nicer furniture.

"In a few days she'll be offered a better job, as

long as she keeps showing up on time and being polite," George explained. "Soon she'll be able to rent a nicer apartment. Don't you worry."

It only took a couple minutes to reach the entrance to the virtual River Heights Mall. Inside, the mall looked incredibly realistic: familiar-looking stores with slightly different names carried all sorts of clothes in the latest styles while gift stores, toy stores, and specialty stores filled in the remaining stalls. Airy, skylighted spaces encouraged shoppers to linger, and VirtualNancy passed three huge, beautiful fountains on the way to the food court.

"The food court is where the action is," George advised us. "It's where all the characters hang out."

I cast a suspicious glance her way. "You don't hang out in the middle-school community of BetterLife, do you?"

George rolled her eyes. "Of course not. But all the River Heights communities are configured to look the same—except for the university, because that's made to look like a campus. You don't think the creators have time to program individual worlds for each community in each city, do you?"

I looked at George blankly.

"Never mind," she said with a sigh. "Anyway, the food court is the place to be."

Virtual Nancy reached a large, open, well-lit space furnished with modern plastic tables and chairs, and filled almost to capacity with chatting teenagers. Along the walls, virtual restaurants offered burgers, Chinese food, tacos, sandwiches, ice cream, and coffee. But it looked like fewer than half the shoppers were actually there to eat; most tables held no food, but all the seats were filled with kids.

"Wow," I murmured breathlessly. "There are so many of them! Does this mean this many middle-school kids are still up playing BetterLife?"

George nodded. "Pretty much," she confirmed. "When you log out, your character kind of goes into survival mode wherever he or she is; she'll still go to work, eat, and sleep, but she won't socialize or go out to entertain herself. Which means all of these characters are being actively controlled."

I shook my head in amazement. There had to be hundreds of kids in the food court—at least half the kids who attended the middle school.

"What do we do?" I asked.

Bess peered at the screen. "Can we sit down at a table and mingle?" she asked. "Maybe some of these kids know about the Shannon situation."

George nodded, and walked over to a nearby table where a few seats were free. Within seconds she'd asked one of the girls there for permission to sit down, and soon VirtualNancy was having a pleasant conversation with two girls and a boy about last night's episode of *America's Next Top Project Runway*, with lots of input from Bess.

I HAVEN'T SEEN U AROUND BEFORE, one of the girls, Junebug67, said to VirtualNancy. R U NEW HERE?

George glanced at me.

"I am," I dictated to her, "but I know Sassy-girl48."

George typed my message out on the keyboard and hit Submit.

The other girl, KylieGal, and the boy, JackOf-All8, abruptly stood up from the table. As they began to walk away, Junebug67 gave me a hasty apology.

SORRY. GTG.

And she left too.

"GTG?" I asked.

"'Got to go,'" supplied Bess, sounding a little exasperated. "Honestly, Nance, even I know that one."

Normally I would have been offended, but a familiar figure had caught my eye in the game. "Wait! Over there, by the yogurt stand. Can you look in that direction?" I asked George, pointing to a familiar blue-streaked head. She clicked a direction on a compass that appeared at the lower right of the screen, then a magnifying glass with a plus sign—the symbol for zooming in. Soon we had a better look at the kids in front of the yogurt shop, and I jumped in my seat.

"That's him!" I cried. "GuitarLvr15! Let's go talk to him!"

George quickly directed VirtualNancy across the food court and over to GuitarLvr15. She clicked on his character and then on a button marked Talk Privately.

"What do I say?" she asked, pausing with her hands over the keyboard.

I swallowed. I actually had no idea how to start a conversation with a virtual middle-school boy.

Luckily Bess jumped into the fray. "Say, 'I'm Nancy. I like the streak in your hair,'" she directed.

George typed that in, then hit Submit.

It seemed like an eternity before my computer beeped, and a message from GuitarLvr15 appeared.

THX. R U NEW HERE?

I glanced at George.

"Yes," she typed. "I just started playing today. What's ur name?"

She glanced over at me, waiting for my approval before she hit Submit. "Good," I said with a nod. "But can we switch places so I can do the talking?"

George smiled and shrugged. "You *are* Real Life Nancy," she agreed.

We switched seats, and just as I sat down, the computer beeped with GutiarLvr15's reply.

MY NAME IS GUITARLVR15. DO U GO 2 RHMS?

I gulped and typed as fast as I could.

I DO. WHAT'S UR REAL NAME?

"Nance," George murmured in a cautious tone.

MY NAME IS GUITARLVR15. WHAT GRADE R U IN?

I wasn't about to accept that as an answer.

8TH GRADE. WHAT'S UR REAL NAME? U CAN TELL ME

George shifted uncomfortably. "You might want to let it go. . . ."

Beep.

MY NAME IS GUITARLVR15. DROP IT. WHAT DO U LIKE 2 DO 4 FUN?

I couldn't let this go.

I LIKE 2 ASK QUESTIONS. WHO R U?? I KNOW JAKE.

I was typing so fast, Bess and George were having trouble keeping up. Just as I hit the Submit button, George jumped up. "Nancy! Don't!"

Within seconds there was a horrible sound, like a car crash or a bomb going off. Suddenly VirtualNancy stood alone in front of the yogurt shop. GuitarLvr15 and his friends had vanished.

A window appeared in the middle of the screen: GUITARLVR15 HAS BLOCKED YOU FROM TALKING TO HIM.

"What??" I cried.

Bess looked crushed as George sighed. "It's a feature of the game," George explained. "You can block anyone from privately talking to you for twenty-four hours."

My mouth hung open. "But then . . . How—

how do Shannon's harassers manage it?" I asked. On-screen, more and more people were walking away from VirtualNancy. I wondered how much of that was due to my interaction with Guitar-Lvr15, and how much was due to the fact that I'd told someone I was a friend of Sassygirl48. "Couldn't she have just blocked them?"

George shook her head. "It's a design flaw in the game. Blocking only applies to private conversations. You can still e-mail someone—everyone has an e-mail address listed in their profile—or you can say something publicly. That's how Shannon's bullies operate."

I sighed, pushing back from the desk and crossing my arms in front of my chest. Poor Virtual-Nancy was an outcast at the mall. My first foray into the virtual world had been a failure. "I think I'm ready to log out and come back to the real world," I muttered.

I stood up, and George took over to log out VirtualNancy and close my Internet browser. "I'll leave you basic directions, Nancy," she offered. "You can get on again tomorrow or whenever you have time, and hopefully you'll have better luck."

I nodded as Bess and George both stood up and

started collecting their things. "I hope so," I said. "Because days might go by fast in the BetterLife world, but I bet time feels like it's crawling for poor Shannon."

FRIEND TO ENEMY?

My cell phone woke me up way too early the next morning. Bess, George, and I had played with VirtualNancy until far later than my usual bedtime, and I was zapped. But when I fished my phone off the nightstand and saw that it was Ned calling, I had to pick up.

"Hello?"

"Don't tell me you're still in bed, Nance," Ned greeted me with a chuckle.

"It's that obvious, huh?" I struggled to sit up in bed, and cleared my throat to get the frogs out.

Ned laughed. "Let's just say it's clear you didn't get up for your usual sunrise jog this morning, okay?"

I smiled. Ned knew me pretty well; he knew

that at sunrise, jogging was about the *last* place he could expect me to be. "What's up?" I asked. "Or were you just calling to say hello?"

"*Actually* I do have a reason," Ned replied. "I'm going to a lecture here at the university tonight, and I thought you might like to join me. It's not the most romantic date night, I know, but maybe we could get dessert afterward?"

"That sounds fun," I replied. "What's the lecture about?"

"It's being given by these two Internet entrepreneurs. Their names are Robert Sung and Jack Crilley. Have you heard of them?"

Robert Sung and Jack Crilley. I searched my brain. "Um, no."

"They created something called BetterLife," Ned explained. "It's a virtual world game that you play on the Internet. You create a character, and then—"

"You control this character's life through the game," I supplied. "Get a job, a place to live, socialize. Oh, I know all about BetterLife."

"You do?" Ned sounded surprised. "Don't take this the wrong way, Nancy, but I didn't have you pegged as an online gamer."

I laughed. "Um, not quite." Tossing back my covers, I swung my legs off the bed and stretched.

"But in the last couple days? Let's just say I got a crash course. I will *definitely* join you for that lecture tonight."

Ned and I chatted for a few more minutes, talking about Shannon's case, the subscription plan for BetterLife, and, finally, how Arij and Ibrahim were faring at school (well, it seemed). After a few minutes Ned had to run to a class, and I decided it was time for me to shower and start my day . . . with a visit to Shannon Fitzgerald.

It was Saturday and relatively early, so I was pretty sure Shannon would still be at home. Nonetheless, I texted her to make sure it was okay.

SURE, she texted back. EAGER 2 HEAR WHAT U'VE FOUND OUT.

I took my time driving over to her house, wondering if she'd be so eager to hear about what I'd found out if she knew that her crush had described her as a mean girl and a bully. I still wasn't 100 percent sure that Jake was a reliable source of information, and I wanted to give Shannon the benefit of the doubt. Besides, Maggie had described her as a nice, well-liked girl. I figured I needed to ask Shannon some questions myself.

"Hi, Nancy," Shannon greeted me cheerfully as

she led the way up to her room. She was dressed in a comfy-looking track suit, with her cornsilk-blond hair piled into a messy bun at the top of her head. She looked more natural than sparkly with no makeup on, but it was still clear that Shannon was a beauty. And from what I remembered of middle school, it still struck me as strange that *she* was the target of bullies.

Shannon opened her bedroom door to reveal a petite, curly haired brunette lounging on her bed, flipping through magazines. "This is my best friend Rebecca," Shannon introduced. "We had a sleepover last night. Hope you don't mind she's here, but Rebecca's like my sister—anything I know, she knows."

I nodded and gave Rebecca a little smile. "Hi, Rebecca," I greeted her. "I'm sure Shannon appreciates you sticking by her through this tough time."

Rebecca widened her eyes. "I *know*, right?" she asked, shaking her head with disbelief. "Some kids can be so cruel. I used to love playing BetterLife. But I just don't get it."

Shannon gestured to her iPod, which was sitting on her desk, connected to some shiny pink speakers. "Rebecca brought over music by this new band. What did you say they were called?"

Rebecca smiled. "Flat Macaroon," she replied. "Aren't they amazing?"

I tuned in to the music. It *was* nice—a mellow arrangement of guitars and synthesizers with a smooth-voiced lead singer crooning about springtime. It was an interesting choice for someone Rebecca's age—a little more sophisticated than I would have expected. "I like it," I agreed. "What's this song called?"

"'Blue in the Springtime,'" Rebecca replied. She shuffled off the bed and walked over to the iPod. "Here. I can turn it off, though, so you guys can talk."

We all took a seat on Shannon's bed, and she looked at me expectantly. "So?" she prompted. "What have you found out?"

I sighed. "Well, there's good news and bad news," I replied. "The main thing I learned is, Jake Seltzer isn't GuitarLvr15."

Shannon and Rebecca turned to each other, mouths dropping open.

"But he *has* to be!" cried Rebecca, shaking her head. "The blue streak! The music thing! Who else could it be?"

I shook my head. "The thing is, he does play BetterLife, but not in the middle-school community. He has a character in the university game that looks nothing like him. He showed me himself."

Shannon suddenly turned pink. "You talked to him about me?" she asked.

I nodded. "Well . . . yeah. I had to find out whether it was really him. And I showed him GuitarLvr15 in the game, but he said he has no idea who they really are, or why they would steal his look. He also seemed honestly surprised by what you're going through."

Shannon looked confused. "But . . . but . . . the things he said when we flirted. . . ."

"He says that wasn't him," I said, reaching out to touch Shannon's arm.

If Shannon looked mortified by this information, Rebecca looked almost angry. "Could he be lying?" she asked me pointedly. "I mean, isn't it likely that if he was making Shannon's life miserable, he wouldn't just come out and tell you?"

I sighed. "He could be," I allowed, "but I believe him. His reactions when we spoke seemed genuine. Shannon"—I turned to her and softened my voice—"when you flirted with GuitarLvr15 . . . That conversation . . . Do you remember him saying anything concrete, anything that would make you think it *definitely* had to be Jake flirting with you?"

Shannon looked lost. "No," she admitted, biting her lip. "I mean, at the time, signs all seemed to say it was definitely him. I was just so *sure*. But looking back . . ." She looked up at her ceiling, trying to remember, then sighed and looked down at her comforter. "Everything I remember for sure . . . Now I realize it could have been anybody." She swallowed. "Or anybody who wanted me to *think* I was talking to Jake."

I nodded, thinking this over. Shannon seemed truly crushed. It was hard to reconcile this fresh-looking, vulnerable tween with the manipulative girl Jake Seltzer had described to me. But I had to ask.

"Shannon," I said gently. "In the course of investigating the case I've heard . . . something else. Something I need to run by you."

Shannon turned to me, looking a little unsure. "Okay," she agreed. "Anything. Go ahead."

"Someone told me . . ." I sighed. "Someone told me you could be mean to the less popular girls in your grade."

Shannon's vulnerable look quickly turned to surprise—and then anger. "What?" she asked. "Who? *Who* told you that?"

I shook my head. "That doesn't matter," I replied. "One story they told me was that you tripped a girl named Sarah O'Malley in the cafeteria. You called her a teacher's pet, because a teacher had read her essay aloud in class."

Shannon looked stunned. "That's—that's ridiculous!" she stammered.

"*Totally* ridiculous," Rebecca agreed, looking even angrier than before. "Shannon would never! What a stupid thing for someone to do!"

"Look," I said, holding up my hand for quiet. "I'm not judging you. No matter what you did, nobody deserves to be treated the way you're being treated. But if it *did* happen, if you *did* act less than nice to someone at school, that may lead to some suspects. Maybe someone is mad at you and trying to get you back."

Shannon scowled but turned to Rebecca, seeming to consider this.

"Look, it's just not true," Rebecca insisted. She'd looked friendly when I first entered the room, but now she was looking at me like I was lower than dirt. "Sarah did trip in the cafeteria. But she tripped over her own two feet, then blamed Shannon. It just really stinks that this rumor actually made it around school and got to whoever you talked to."

"It's true," Shannon confirmed. "I would never, in my life, be that mean to someone on purpose. I can't believe people are spreading lies about me! Why would I need to act like that to feel cool?"

I looked from Shannon to Rebecca and back, trying to take all this in. They both looked utterly sure of themselves. So sure, in fact, it made me suspicious. It almost seemed like they were getting *too* defensive. I didn't know what to believe.

Shannon's eyes narrowed as she studied my face. "You don't believe me, do you?"

I was caught off guard. "That's not it, I—"

But Shannon didn't miss a beat. "You can ask her yourself," she went on coldly. "Sarah and I used to take dance class together on Saturday mornings. I know she's still in the class. It's down in the shopping center on River Street, and it lets out at eleven. She has long, dark hair and green eyes." She glanced at her watch. "If you hurry, you can just make it."

I glanced at my watch: 10:39. The River Street Shopping Center was about fifteen minutes away. I had an uneasy feeling about this—Rebecca and Shannon were still giving me a strange vibe—but it *did* seem like the easiest way to resolve who was telling the truth: Jake or Shannon. And once I knew that, I'd have a better idea who might be the bully here.

I stood up. "I'll do that," I agreed. "It's not that I don't trust you. It's just—"

"You'd better hurry," Shannon cut me off, leaning back on her bed and fixing me with an icy look. "You don't want to miss her."

I grabbed my purse and headed for the door.

"*Buh*-bye," Rebecca called after me, reaching over to turn the iPod back on.

Nice. I hurried down the stairs and out the front door, shaking my head as I unlocked my car and settled myself in the driver's seat.

How had I somehow become the villain?

The River Street Shopping Center was a fancy name for a ragtag strip mall a few blocks from downtown River Heights. Sammie Lee's Dance Studio was on the far right, and as I drove into the parking lot at 10:56, I could see the class still stretching to the rhythm of a slow ballad.

I let out my breath, realizing then that I'd been holding it for a while. I made it!

As I pulled into a space facing the mirror-lined studio, I could tell the music had stopped and class was coming to an end. Girls stretched and started gathering their things, stopping to chat in small groups. I spotted one girl wearing a black leotard, pink-striped tights, and purple leg warmers; her chestnut-colored hair was tied in a messy bun at her neck. She looked flushed and happy as she chatted with a curly-haired redhead and a pretty Asian girl. She walked over and grabbed a purple backpack from a communal pile at the front of the room; fishing around in it, she pulled out a small cell phone and started clicking through messages. Her smile faded as she became focused on her phone and her green eyes grew serious.

That has to be her. Sarah O'Malley. I sighed, turning off my car's engine and opening my door. Would Sarah be cooperative?

I climbed out of my car and strolled over to the dance studio's entrance. Girls were already spilling out, talking and laughing. Some of them glanced my way curiously, but nobody said anything. Finally, the girl I'd pegged as Sarah walked out, a serious look on her face as she scanned the parking lot, probably looking for her ride.

"Hey!" I called, trying to get her attention. "Are you Sarah?"

She glanced at me. Interestingly she didn't look all that surprised. "I am," she said warily. "Who are you?"

"I'm Nancy." I smiled, trying to seem friendly. "Can I talk to you for a second? I just have a couple questions to ask."

Sarah glanced at the parking lot one more time, and shrugged. "Sure," she said. "My ride's not here yet."

"Let's sit over there." I gestured to a picnic table that sat in a small area of grass outside a barbecue joint. Sarah nodded and we walked over. She didn't seem all that enthused to talk to me, but she didn't quite seem annoyed, either.

We sat and I smiled again. "Listen, I'm sorry to bother you. It's just that I've been talking to a classmate of yours, Shannon Fitzgerald?"

"Sure, Shannon." Sarah nodded to let me know she knew Shannon, but her expression gave away nothing. I couldn't tell if Shannon was a close friend or an enemy—or someone Sarah only passed occasionally in the hallway.

"You may know this already," I continued, "but Shannon is being harassed online. In a game called BetterLife. Do you know it?"

Sarah shrugged. "I've heard of it," she said simply. "I'm not much for online gaming."

"Okay." I paused. "Listen, I'll get to the point of why I'm talking to you . . . I was told by who I thought was a reliable source that Shannon can be a little mean to other girls at school."

Sarah blinked and looked down at the table. She didn't look very excited to talk about this subject.

"Specifically," I went on, undaunted, "I was told that there was an incident between the two of you in the cafeteria. That a teacher of yours had read your essay out loud in class that day, and Shannon called you a teacher's pet and tripped you." I paused again. Sarah was still staring at the table, stone-faced. "In front of everyone," I added.

Sarah was silent for almost a minute before she spoke, so quietly I could barely hear her. She looked past me, toward the parking lot. "You heard wrong," she told me.

"What do you mean?" I pressed. "It never happened at all? Or someone misheard what happened?"

Sarah swallowed, but didn't look up. "You misheard it," she said. "I tripped myself. I can be clumsy. Shannon had nothing to do with it."

She still wouldn't look me in the eye. It was unnerving. "Nothing at all?" I asked.

"Nothing at all." Sarah finally looked up, frowning at me. "Was there anything else? My mom's going to be here any minute."

Was there anything else? No, not really, except that I was getting a funny vibe from Sarah. Something seemed off about her story, something I couldn't quite put my finger on.

"Nothing else," I replied, flashing a bright smile as I glanced into my purse. "Well, actually, I *do* have another question for you, but it has nothing to do with Shannon."

Sarah actually smiled a little bit, looking relieved. "Okay," she agreed. "What is it?"

"Can I borrow your cell phone?" I asked hopefully, giving her a little just-between-us-girls smile. "I told my boyfriend I'd give him a call to set up our date tonight, and then I stupidly left my phone at home." I shook my head. "Do you have one? I promise it will only take a second."

Sarah shrugged. "Oh, sure." She reached into her purse and pulled out a metallic-purple cell phone. "But once my mom comes, I'll need to go."

"No problem," I said, nodding. "I'll be fast. I just need to get the address of the restaurant where I'm meeting him from my car."

I walked over to my car with Sarah's phone, then opened the door and climbed into the driver's seat, trying to look like I was searching for a piece of paper. Actually, though, I wanted to get a better look at Sarah's cell phone. I have lots of experience snooping on different kinds of phones, but it took me a few tries to locate the Sent/Received Texts option on Sarah's.

Finally I found it. Sent Texts. There was nothing recent. Received Texts. There was just one today, from a familiar-looking number.

IF N E 1 ASKS. . . U BETTER NOT SAY N E THING ABOUT WHAT HAPPENED IN THE CAFTERIA. U TRIPPED URSELF, U KLUTZ.

It was from Shannon.

For a moment I just sat there and stared at the text, amazed. So Shannon really did have a "mean streak," as Jake had put it. She had tripped Sarah in the cafeteria. . . . And worse, Sarah was frightened enough of Shannon to lie for her about it.

What kind of person was I working for?

I bit my lip, glancing at Sarah, who still sat at the picnic table. She stared down at the sleeve of her hoodie as she picked at a loose thread. She looked unhappy. I decided not to say anything to her about the text. She didn't strike me as the cyberbullying type, and goodness knew Shannon had her pretty freaked out if that text was any indication.

I got out of my car and walked back to the picnic table. Feeling jittery, I started flipping the tiny cell phone over and over in my hand.

"Thanks," I told Sarah when I reached her. "You're a lifesaver." I held her cell phone out to her.

And then I saw it, on the back of the phone.

A shiny decal: a Celtic knot.

Just like the girl who had harassed Shannon in BetterLife.

MAKING ENEMIES

I decided not to say anything to Sarah about the Celtic knot decal. It wasn't enough evidence to really accuse her of anything, and I wanted to have more information before I confronted anyone. That night, I met Ned in the lobby outside of the university auditorium, eager to learn more about the two creators of BetterLife.

"Nancy!" Ned cried as he spotted me through the huge and growing crowd. Apparently we weren't the only two people interested in hearing what Robert Sung and Jack Crilley had to say. "I'm so glad to see you. Listen, I—"

"Nancy?" A familiar, friendly, accented voice

piped up behind Ned, and soon Ibrahim maneuvered around some university students to join us. "How nice to see you again! How have you been?"

"Hi, Nancy!" No sooner had Ibrahim appeared than his sister Arij popped up behind him.

"The outfit you helped me pick out for my first day was a big hit! But I may need your advice again. Fashion is very complicated in middle school."

I smiled at Ibrahim and Arij, honestly happy to see them but also a little surprised.

"I'm sorry, Nance," Ned murmured, taking my arm and swiftly leaning up to whisper in my ear. "I wasn't planning on bringing them, but when I mentioned the lecture, they seemed so intrigued by it. They don't know many people in town yet, and I think they're suffering from a little cabin fever. I know this isn't the date we planned on."

"It's fine," I whispered back, squeezing Ned's arm. "We'll make up for it later." I turned to Ibrahim and Arij, raising my voice to its normal level. "It's good to see you two again! How's school going?"

After fifteen minutes of updates—it seemed both Ibrahim and Arij were *really* enjoying their time in the River Heights school system—we all settled into a center row about halfway back from the stage.

"So explain this to me again," Ibrahim said brightly, looking at the huge crowd around us. "What is BetterLife and why is it so popular?"

Ibrahim looked expectantly at me, but it was Ned who replied first.

"It's an online community," he explained, "a virtual world game. You create a character and control everything about him or her, including his job and living situation. But most people use BetterLife to socialize. You can hang out and meet people just like in real life, but from the comfort of your own home."

Arij nodded, looking fascinated. "And do you and Nancy have these BetterLife characters?" she asked.

"Well—" I started, at the same time Ned replied, "I do, but I don't play very often."

I turned around in surprise. "You *do*?" I asked Ned, who looked a little sheepish. "I didn't realize you played BetterLife. Are you part of the university community?"

Ned shrugged. "When I started at the university," he explained, "*everyone* was getting on BetterLife. I figured I'd give it a try. It's fun, but I never really got into it like a lot of people."

I was still a little surprised that my boyfriend, who doesn't spend much time online by any means—had a secret online identity. "And you—did you meet people through BetterLife?" I asked.

"Occasionally. Just as friends, though, sometimes with similar interests. That's one nice thing about the online community: It makes it very easy to find people who have common interests."

Hmm. I knew I shouldn't be jealous. Ned is the most trustworthy guy I know. Still, I wondered how I had missed out on this whole BetterLife bandwagon.

"You said you played too?" Arij asked, turning to me.

"Oh." I pulled my thoughts back to the present, and turned to Arij with a smile. "I actually just created a character to help me investigate a case I'm working on. So I'm still a newbie."

"A noob . . .?" Ibrahim frowned, perplexed by the unfamiliar vocabulary.

"I'm sorry. I'm still new at it, is what I meant," I clarified.

"It sounds like a wonderful idea," Arij murmured, looking excited.

"It does," Ibrahim agreed. "I would like very

much to go home and try this game myself! It sounds like a good way to meet friends in a new town."

"Oh," I said, shaking my head quickly, "I'm not sure about that, Ibrahim. People can be cruel online. And it's very easy to lie about your identity, so not everybody is what they seem."

Ibrahim shrugged. "Isn't that true in real life, also?" he asked. "You might think that someone is your friend, when in fact they say terrible things about you when you're not around. Or perhaps someone lies about liking opera to seem smarter. Everyone has secrets."

"But I—" I started to argue with Ibrahim, but stopped myself. He *did* have a point. And surely Ibrahim and Arij would be careful online. They both seemed like smart kids.

"Oh look," Ned said, nodding toward a trio of men who were stepping onto the stage. "I think that's them—Jack Crilley and Robert Sung. And there's my computer-science professor to introduce them."

A bearded, salt-and-pepper-haired man stepped up to the microphone. "Greetings," he announced. "I want to thank everyone for coming tonight. I'm Professor Frank of the computer-science department, and I'm here to introduce two men who have revolutionized the way we socialize with one another, make friends, and express ourselves to an increasingly diverse Internet population. Who here has a character on BetterLife?"

Almost the entire audience raised their hands. "Wow," Ibrahim whispered to me.

"Before BetterLife," Professor Frank continued, "socializing on the Internet was largely limited to impersonal and difficult-to-police chatrooms, and social networking sites where your entire persona is represented by a two-dimensional, text-heavy profile." He smiled, turning to glance at the BetterLife entrepreneurs. "Robert Sung and Jack Crilley changed all that. Now, through BetterLife, everyone can live a complete, three-dimensional life on the Internet. Sometimes, as the name suggests, a life that is even better than the 'real' one. As many of you know, in three weeks BetterLife will begin to offer a subscription service, so that users can pay for an enhanced online experience. It is estimated that more than five million users will pay for this service, making our two guests very rich men." The two young entrepreneurs chuckled uncomfortably, and Professor Frank glanced at them and laughed too. "Many of the students in this auditorium will probably soon be turning over a bigger portion of their paychecks to these two inventors. Ladies and gentlemen, I give you two visionaries: Robert Sung and Jack Crilley."

The applause was almost deafening as the two surprisingly young men—a small Asian man with a goatee and a taller, gawky redhead—stepped up to the podium.

"Helloooo, BetterLifers!" the redhead, who I assumed to be Jack, cooed into the microphone. The response was amazing. People were yelling and cheering, as if Sung and Crilley were a football team who had just won the Super Bowl, instead of two skinny computer programmers.

I glanced at Ned. "This should be interesting," I whispered.

Ned nodded, looking a little taken aback himself. "Something like that," he agreed.

"So as you can see," Robert Sung was explaining two hours later, after he and Jack had shared with us every detail of their childhoods, adolescence, and early adulthood years. "BetterLife has revolutionized the gaming industry, Internet networking, and, indeed, the way people socialize in general."

"Robert and I are a little uncomfortable with the term *genius*," Jack broke in, trying to look humble, "but we do recognize the importance of what we've done here. Without BetterLife, we would all be limited by the scope of our off-line—some would say *real*, but we don't believe interactions in BetterLife are any less real—lives."

The duo was quiet for just a moment, and for what seemed like the thousandth time that night, applause swept through the auditorium. I caught Ned's eye.

"You would think they were rock stars!" I muttered.

Ned nodded. "Or they just announced that we're skipping midterms this year," he whispered back.

I turned to my other side, and saw that Ibrahim and Arij were watching the programmers with starry-eyed expressions.

"It sounds like they have really changed the world, Nancy!" Ibrahim said eagerly, when he caught my glance. "I can't wait to get home to create my character."

"Me too!" Arij agreed.

"You two just be careful on there," I whispered. "In this game, you can't be sure anything is what it seems."

Finally the applause died down, and Robert

moved toward the microphone again. "Are there any questions?"

I threw my hand in the air. I certainly had a few questions for these two. After listening to two hours of how brilliant and dedicated and revolutionary BetterLife was, I wanted to hear what they had to say about a few of its flaws.

Unfortunately for me, many other members of the audience had questions, too. They ranged from, "How can you tell when someone's hitting on you in BetterLife?" to "In the university community, in the science building cafeteria, what is the code to get two drumsticks instead of one? My friend did it once, and I've never been able to figure out how."

Robert and Jack seemed flattered, and were patient with everybody. Many of the questions from the audience ended with, ". . . and I just think you two are brilliant," so I don't exactly think the Q & A was hard on their already-healthy egos.

"You there, in the yellow sweater," Jack said finally, pointing in my direction. "With the reddish hair. What was your question?"

I stood up. "What is your feeling on the lack of background checks in BetterLife?" I asked.

The two young men just stared at each other

blankly, as though I'd asked my question in Martian. "Background checks?" asked Robert. "I'm not sure what you mean. People are playing a game here, not running for political office."

A chuckle ran through the crowd.

"I *mean*," I replied, "that it's very easy to misrepresent yourself on BetterLife. You can change your age, your gender, even your appearance. I could log on right now as a sixty-year-old square dancer from Philadelphia, and you would never know I was anything different."

Jack actually looked annoyed at my comment. "Well, miss," he replied sharply, "that's part of the *game* of BetterLife. It wouldn't be a better life if it were the exact same one you were already living, would it?"

Again, the crowd chuckled. I stood my ground, though, waiting for more of a response. Finally Jack continued.

"On BetterLife, people can try out other ages, genders, identities. It's a game. And I don't know who you are, miss, but the Internet is a free society that will police itself. If a game becomes unpleasant to play, people will stop playing and the website will die. Neither Robert nor I would feel comfortable violating our members' privacies with these 'background checks' you're talking about, so they're not going to happen. And I think somehow our members will be just fine. Next question?"

"Wait!" I cried, holding up my hand. "Doesn't allowing people to create new identities with no accountability encourage people to be cruel to one another, to do and say things they'd never get away with in real life?" I asked. "If we met on the street, I would never call you a horrible name because you might see me again; you might tell other people I know that I behaved badly. But in the game, if I'm hiding behind some made-up identity, why couldn't I be cruel to you? Or anybody? By the time you figure out who I am, I'll already have created an entirely new character."

Jack shook his head, looking disgusted with me. "I'm done here. Next question?"

"*Furthermore,*" I broke in, "when you start your subscription service, you'll have to collect personal information from your members: billing information, credit card numbers, addresses. Why not just use that information when people are being harassed online?"

Jack looked like he'd been sucking on a lemon. He glanced at Robert, who shook his head, and then said curtly, "Clearly some of our audience members don't grasp the idea of freedom and the right to privacy. I think we've answered all the questions we're going to tonight. Thank you for coming."

A buzz of disappointment ran through the crowd as the two programmers suddenly moved away from the microphone and walked offstage. Students turned to one another with disbelief—and to me with disgust.

"Thanks for nothing, weirdo," huffed a blond girl behind me. "I'll never learn how to make my character famous now."

People began gathering their things and moving toward the exits. I turned sheepishly to Ned. "Do you think she meant famous in real life, or famous in the game?" I asked quietly.

Ned just shook his head. "For some of these people, Nance," he replied, "I think there is only the game."

I glanced toward the door. The lecture was being followed by a reception in the lobby, where Robert and Jack were supposed to mingle with the crowd. I hoped that some of the audience would have their questions answered there, but I still wanted *my* question answered also. It wouldn't make anyone happy, but I felt I had to try to speak with Jack and Robert again, and figure out what they really knew about the security lapses in their game.

Ned, Ibrahim, Arij, and I followed the crowd toward the lobby. Ibrahim and Arij kept up a bubbly discourse about the amazing features of BetterLife, and how they planned to control their characters.

"I think Little Arij will be a dancer," Arij was saying. "She'll take lessons three times a week, and hopefully after a few months she will get a job on Broadway."

Ibrahim shook his head. "My character will be just like me," he insisted. "Perhaps taller, and perhaps he will have a mustache. But we will share the same interests and the same personality. That way, everyone I meet in the game can also be my friend in real life."

Ned wrinkled his nose. "A *mustache*, Ibrahim?" he asked. "I think that may be the wrong call."

Ibrahim looked startled. "Perhaps a full beard, then?" he asked. "Or . . . I know. A soul patch?"

Just then I spotted Robert Sung and Jack Crilley, escorted by Professor Frank, trying to quietly enter the lobby through an unmarked door. But within seconds, whispers erupted throughout the crowd and a small mob of adoring fans began to form around them.

"Excuse me," I murmured, wandering away from Ned, Ibrahim, and Arij and trying to angle my way through the crowd to get to the two founders.

"And so, after that, I really had a much easier time meeting people and had much more confidence," a pretty, dark-haired girl with glasses was explaining to Robert and Jack as I stepped closer. "I really credit your game with changing my life."

"That's amazing," Robert replied gently, patting her shoulder. "I really think that—"

Suddenly Jack spotted me in the crowd and began freaking out. "Stop her! Stop! I don't want to talk to her, I don't want to talk to that girl! She was hostile in the Q and A!" He pointed right at me, and Professor Frank looked me over, an uncomfortable expression on his face. Robert also looked uncomfortable. It was like neither one of them really wanted to tell me to get lost, but they didn't know what else to do.

Finally Robert cut through the awkwardness by gently placing a hand on Jack's shoulder. "Come on, Jack," he coaxed. "Let's just hear what she has to say." He turned to me, smiling sheepishly. "Forgive Jack," he apologized. "He's just very passionate about our creation. He can be sensitive to criticism."

I nodded understandingly. "I can see that," I replied. "Look, I don't want to ruin your night. Clearly your creation *has* changed a lot of lives for the better, and no one can take that away."

Both creators nodded, Jack's expression softening a bit. "I appreciate you saying that," he murmured.

"It's just . . . I'm working with a young girl, who's now being harassed and bullied through BetterLife," I explained. "I know the game wasn't invented for this purpose, but it *does* make the whole process much easier, since the game is so anonymous. Almost everyone in the middle school is playing."

Robert nodded. "That's an unfortunate misuse of our game," he said.

"Listen," I coaxed. "This girl is having her house vandalized—in the game—and getting all kinds of private messages and e-mails that contain language I wouldn't wish on my worst enemy." I paused. "I know you want to protect the users' identities, but knowing what's going on in this case, is there any way you could share the identity of the head bully?"

Jack glared at me. "Who says we have it?" he demanded.

I sighed. "I've played BetterLife," I explained.

"I know you take basic contact information from users. Anything you could give us would be helpful to narrow down—"

But Jack was already moving away, shaking his head. "I'm sorry, miss," he replied curtly. "The Internet is a reflection of our society: People are people, and just as people bully in real life, people will bully on the Internet. Logging onto a computer doesn't improve your character."

"But this is worse than—"

Jack scowled, and cut in again. "Robert and I strongly believe in the Internet being a free society," he insisted. "We will not share that information with you, or anyone. Period. I'm leaving now."

He turned to leave the lobby, and I held up my hands. "Forget it. Don't leave on my account," I said, backing away. "*I'll* leave. You guys mingle with your fans." I gestured for the other students and audience members to take my place, and slowly disentangled myself, until I was on the outer reaches of the mob.

"Nancy!" A hand reached out and grabbed my arm, and I turned, relieved to see Ned.

"Hey," I said with a sigh. "Well, I think I just officially—"

But Ned frowned, cutting me off. "Where've

you been?" he asked. "You just wandered off. I've been looking all over for you. I need to get Ibrahim and Arij home. They have school tomorrow."

I glanced behind Ned to see Arij and Ibrahim awkwardly drinking punch and watching our conversation. "I'm so sorry," I said honestly. "I went to ask Robert and Jack some more questions; I thought you heard me."

Ned shrugged. "Never mind," he said, touching my shoulder. "I was hoping we'd get some time alone tonight," he went on, gesturing to Ibrahim and his sister. "But . . ."

I nodded sympathetically, squeezing his arm. "I guess it just wasn't meant to be." I shrugged. "It's okay. We'll make another date, and catch up later."

He leaned over and kissed the tip of my nose. "You're the best, Nance," he said softly, then led me back to Ibrahim and Arij.

Ibrahim was holding a handout from the lecture with a pen poised above it, ready to write something down. "Nancy," he said eagerly, "you have a BetterLife ID, right? Ned said he has one, but it's for the university community. I'd like to keep an eye on Arij, so we would both be joining the middle-school community. That's where you play, right?"

I smiled and nodded. "Sure. It's VirtualNancy. You can look for me at the mall."

Ibrahim grinned, writing on his paper. "You bet I will, VirtualNancy," he said with a smile. "I look forward to having you as a virtual friend."

VIRTUALLY REJECTED

"**N**ancy, come on," Bess was pleading with me the next day, as once again, she, George, and I sat in front of the computer. "It's only twenty dollars, and it would look so cute on you."

"Not *me*," I corrected her. "On VirtualNancy."

Bess tossed her hands in the air. "Real Nancy, virtual Nancy, whoever!" she cried in frustration. "The point is, VirtualNancy is moving up in the world. She has a new job, a new supercute apartment. Don't you think she should treat herself to a new blouse in celebration?"

I paused, looking on my computer screen at a ruffly yellow blouse that hung in the window of

Cute Betty's Online Boutique. It *would* go nicely with VirtualNancy's brown tweed pants, and it'd definitely update her look, but was it necessary?

"She doesn't need it," George insisted. "We should save that twenty dollars and send Virtual-Nancy to that virtual computer class at the virtual community college. We need to invest in her *future*—not just fritter away her money on trendy clothes."

Bess sighed. "You two, I swear," she muttered to herself. "Maybe with some new virtual clothes, VirtualNancy might get herself a virtual *boyfriend*."

"I heard that," I snapped. "And I'm not in this game for love, I'm in it for *information*."

It had been only a few days since the creation of VirtualNancy, and already her life situation had drastically improved. Through careful and diligent game play (I was spending two or three hours online every day), Nancy had advanced from salon janitor to bookstore manager, and from drafty studio apartment to cute one-bedroom condo with a virtual river view. I had to admit, I was proud of her. Me. Us. Whoever. It was a lot more fun playing BetterLife when your character's life was, well, better.

"Oh wow," George murmured, pointing at a

tiny purple dot on-screen. "That's him! Across the food court! It's GuitarLvr15!"

I looked closer, and sure enough, George was right. Although I'd played several times, I hadn't encountered GuitarLvr15 again since that first night in the food court, when he'd blocked me from talking to him. That block had long since expired, but still . . .

"Should I try to talk to him again?" I asked.

"I guess," Bess replied. "I mean, it couldn't hurt, right?"

"Right." Careful to move slowly and not intimidate him, I moved VirtualNancy slowly and casually across the food court floor. It was still driving me crazy: Who *was* GuitarLvr15? Could he be Sarah? She didn't seem that bold, but possibly . . . Could he be Jake, lying about his true motives? Or could he be someone else entirely?

HI, I had VirtualNancy remark casually to GuitarLvr15. YOU LOOK NICE 2DAY. WANT 2 GET SOMETHING 2 EAT?

It only took a few seconds before GuitarLvr15 began moving away. He made no indication of having received my message, but it was clear that he had. Why else would he move across the food court so suddenly? Clearly, even if the twenty-four-hour block had worn off, Guitar-Lvr15's wariness of VirtualNancy had not.

"Ugh," I muttered to my friends, sighing. "What do we do now? He's the whole reason I'm playing this game, and he won't talk to me."

"Uh, Nance," George replied, pointing at the screen again. "Do you know this kid?"

I looked where her finger pointed, and spotted a tall, skinny, olive-skinned boy with short, dark hair and a triangle-shape patch of stubble on his chin. Suddenly it came to me.

"Ibrahim!" I had VirtualNancy greet him.

NANCY! I WAS COMING TO SAY HELLO TO YOU. HOW ARE YOU? HOW DO YOU LIKE BETTERIBRAHIM4?

I chuckled.

I STILL LIKE THE REAL IBRAHIM BETTER, BUT HE'S PRETTY IMPRESSIVE. ARE YOU HAVING FUN?

It only took a few seconds for Ibrahim to respond.

DEFINITELY. I LIKE THIS GAME VERY MUCH. EVERYONE IS SO FRIENDLY. ARE YOU HAVING FUN, NANCY?

I sighed. "I would be," I typed, then quickly deleted it, deciding not to explain the whole GuitarLvr15 situation to Ibrahim. But then an idea came to me.

I AM HAVING FUN, I typed, BUT I COULD USE A FAVOR IF YOU'RE NOT BUSY.

This time he responded even faster.

ANYTHING FOR YOU, NANCY.

"What are you up to?" Bess asked, casting a suspicious glance my way.

"Isn't this Ned's little houseguest?" asked George. "What do you think he could do for us?"

I began typing.

THERE'S A BOY OVER THERE CALLED GUITARLVR15. I NEED TO KNOW WHO HE REALLY IS, BUT HE WON'T TALK TO ME, BECAUSE HE DOESN'T TRUST ME. HE DOESN'T KNOW YOU, THOUGH. COULD YOU TRY TALKING TO HIM?

It only took a few seconds for Ibrahim's reply to light up my screen.

OF COURSE! I WOULD BE HAPPY TO HELP.

We chatted a bit more, and I briefed Ibrahim on what I needed to know and how to approach GuitarLvr15 without seeming suspicious. We made arrangements to meet in a nearby virtual park, so I could leave immediately and Guitar-Lvr15 wouldn't see me hanging around. As I guided VirtualNancy out of the mall, across the street and onto a park bench, George looked at me skeptically.

"Do you think that's a good idea?" she asked. "Involving him like this?"

I shrugged. "I think I need to use all of the tools at my disposal," I replied. "Besides, Ibrahim is really friendly. I'm not asking him to act out of character by chatting someone up."

George sighed. "I guess you're right," she agreed. "Besides, it's not like VirtualNancy was having a lot of luck."

It was about twenty minutes, real-world time, before BetterIbrahim4 came to meet VirtualNancy at BetterLife Park. George, Bess, and I passed the time by catching up and throwing out ideas for who GuitarLvr15 might be. Unfortunately, besides the absurd guesses—the mayor! Hannah! Bess's mom!—we didn't really have a clue. I was beginning to fear this case just might be unsolvable. How do you catch a virtual crook?

Finally BetterIbrahim4 approached.

HI THERE, I greeted him. HOW DID IT GO?

BetterIbrahim4 shook his head. NOT SO GOOD, he replied. GUITARLVR15 IS VERY TOUCHY ABOUT BEING QUESTIONED, NO?

I pressed the button to make VirtualNancy nod. I SHOULD HAVE WARNED YOU.

Ibrahim explained that his conversation with GuitarLvr15 had started out friendly, with the two exchanging names, ages, hobbies, that sort of thing. GuitarLvr15 told BetterIbrahim4 that he was really into music, and even deejayed sometimes at virtual BetterLife parties. He recommended a few bands BetterIbrahim4 might like, and asked him how he was enjoying the game so far. But when Ibrahim asked his true identity, under the guise of wanting to hang out in real life, GuitarLvr15 turned cold.

I'M GUITARLVR15, he'd told Ibrahim. THAT'S ALL THAT MATTERS.

When Ibrahim pressed on, GuitarLvr15 had threatened him. U'D BETTER DROP IT IF U KNOW WHAT'S GOOD 4 U, he'd said. NOT EVERYONE IN THIS GAME IS AS FRIENDLY AS I AM.

"Is he threatening to have Ibrahim beaten up?" I asked Bess and George, in real life, in the comfort of my bedroom.

Bess shook her head. "I think he's threatening to have *virtual* Ibrahim *virtually* beaten up," she corrected.

"Gosh," I muttered. "This is confusing."

"Although that's sort of what's happening to Shannon, right?" George asked, gesturing to the screen. "She's being seriously harassed online, and it's getting just as bad as being bullied in real life."

"That's true," I agreed, considering. "So if GuitarLvr15 is threatening virtual Ibrahim, I guess that's further evidence that he's a cyberbully. Maybe he harasses a lot of people online, not just Shannon."

I'M SORRY I COULDN'T GET MORE INFORMATION FOR YOU, NANCY, BetterIbrahim4 was apologizing online.

THAT'S OKAY, I typed. I WISH WE COULD FIGURE OUT WHO HE IS, BUT I APPRECIATE YOU TRYING.

Suddenly BetterIbrahim4 whipped a piece of paper out from his jeans pocket. BUT ALL IS NOT LOST! he exclaimed.

?, I typed.

WHEN WE FIRST STARTED CHATTING, Ibrahim explained, GUITARLVR15 GAVE ME THIS FLYER.

I directed VirtualNancy to take the flyer and look at it. The contents took over my screen:

FRIDAY NIGHT SOCIAL AT SAM'S SMOOTHIE SHACK! COME GET YOUR GROOVE ON AT 9 PM THIS FRIDAY NIGHT. ENJOY FREE SNACKS, DELICIOUS SMOOTHIES, AND SLAMMIN' TUNES SPUN BY OUR HOUSE DJ, GUITARLVR15. DON'T BE SHY—YOU MIGHT MAKE SOME NEW FRIENDS!

Simple illustrations of music notes, a smoothie, and dancing kids decorated the sides.

HE IS DEEJAYING FRIDAY NIGHT, Ibrahim explained. MAYBE IF YOU GO TO THE PARTY, YOU WILL LEARN SOMETHING USEFUL.

"He's right," George agreed. "It couldn't hurt to observe GuitarLvr15 in a more social setting. Maybe you'll get some clues."

"Good idea," I agreed, thanking Ibrahim on-screen. "I guess I have a date with my computer then."

I said good-bye to BetterIbrahim4, then set VirtualNancy on the path home so I could get some dinner in her and put her to bed. She had to work early the next morning; no more time for socializing tonight. As we passed by a playground, though, I spotted a familiar character out of the corner of my eye.

"That's her!" I cried. "The bully with the Celtic knot tattoo that looks just like the decal on Sarah's phone!"

I directed VirtualNancy into her path, and Bess

looked uneasy. "Are you sure you have enough evidence to . . ."

SARAH, I typed, addressing ILoveDublin. IS THAT YOU? Several seconds went by before I got a response.

WHO'S ASKING?

I bit my lip. I KNOW WHAT REALLY HAPPENED WITH SHANNON, I wrote. YOU CAN TRUST ME. Taking a deep breath, I positioned the mouse over the Send button and clicked.

Crash. That horrible sound effect blared once more, and a window came up: ILOVEDUBLIN HAS BLOCKED YOU FROM TALKING TO HER.

The girl with the Celtic knot tattoo was gone, and VirtualNancy stood alone on an empty street.

"You know," I said to Bess and George, "I think I may just come across better in real life."

BULLIES AND VICTIMS

After a few more fruitless BetterLife games—where VirtualNancy was promoted once more, and bought a really nifty hybrid convertible, but learned nothing more about GuitarLvr15—I was ready to go back to sleuthing the old-fashioned way: by asking questions in person.

And so I climbed into my car and headed to Bess's house.

As I parked in Bess's driveway, my phone beeped twice, indicating two new text messages. I was happy to see that the first was from Ned.

DINNER TONIGHT? FLAVIO'S, JUST YOU AND ME?

I smiled. A cozy dinner at our favorite Italian restaurant sounded like the perfect night to me. MEET YOU THERE AT 8? I texted back.

YOU'RE ON, Ned replied after a few seconds. CAN'T WAIT TO SEE YOU.

Trying to wipe the dopey smile off my face, I checked the second text message. It was from Shannon.

R U EVER GOING TO SOLVE THIS? SCHOOL IS SOO HARD.

Well, that wiped the smile off my face. It also reminded me that I still had no clue who Guitar-Lvr15 was, or how I would find out. Typing quickly, I made arrangements to meet Shannon at her house later that afternoon. Hopefully I would have some more information by then. If not, I could probably spend at least an hour telling Shannon all the things I *didn't* know.

Shoving my phone into my purse, I climbed out of my car and headed to the door, lightly pressing the doorbell. After a few seconds, Bess appeared. "Hey," she greeted me. "She's in the kitchen, waiting."

I followed Bess down the short hallway to their small, warm yellow kitchen. Maggie was sitting at the table, engrossed in the very activity I'd just been involved in: furious texting. I was amazed as I watched her fingers fly over the tiny keys of her cell phone. Texting was definitely an art I hadn't quite mastered yet.

"Hi, Maggie," I greeted her.

She glanced up. "Oh, hi, Nancy," she said with a crooked smile. "Bess said you wanted to talk to me?"

I nodded, sitting next to her at the table. Bess offered me a drink or a snack, but I declined. "I have a few questions for you," I said to Maggie.

"Okay," she replied, looking a little nervous.

"Before we start, I just want to be clear," I cautioned her, "there are no wrong answers here, okay? I just need you to be completely honest. If I'm going to help your friend Shannon, I need to have all the information."

Maggie nodded slightly, looking a little caught off guard. "Um, okay," she replied.

"I need to know the truth," I said, looking Maggie in the eye. "Is Shannon *ever* mean to people at school?"

Maggie bit her lip. "She's not, not really," she said after a few seconds. "I mean, people take her the wrong way sometimes. But when you get to know Shannon, you see how totally great she is!"

"Okay," I said quietly. "So Shannon can be

misunderstood. Can I ask you about a specific incident, though?"

Maggie shrugged. "Sure, if you want."

I leaned a little closer. "Did Shannon trip a girl named Sarah O'Malley in the cafeteria?" I asked.

Maggie looked horribly uncomfortable. Finally she looked down at the table. "Yeah," she said, as though I was torturing this out of her. "But it wasn't as bad as people made it out to be. Besides, Sarah totally had it coming!"

"Maggie!" cried Bess sharply, looking concerned. "How on Earth would you have something like that coming?"

"Sarah totally stole Shannon's *boyfriend*!" Maggie replied, a little triumphantly.

"Wait a minute, wait a minute," I broke in, trying to replay everything Shannon had told me in my mind. I could swear she'd never said anything about having a *boyfriend*. "Who was this boyfriend? A boy at school?"

Maggie nodded her head. "Yeah, but he was older," she replied. "He's sixteen. He works at the coffee shop downtown."

I frowned. "Jake Seltzer?" I asked.

"Yeah, that's him."

I sighed, glancing at Bess. "Jake wasn't Shannon's boyfriend," I corrected Maggie.

But Maggie just looked at me pityingly. "Not *officially*," she replied, and I could suddenly hear Shannon's voice in every syllable. "But he was totally into her. They had a thing. It was only a matter of time before they started going out."

I glanced at Bess. Her expression told me that she was having the same reaction I was: This did not sound like Maggie. Was she just parroting what Shannon had told her?

"Okay," I said, deciding not to press the issue. "You said that Sarah made a move on him? How did that happen?"

Maggie gave me a confidential look. "She used to go to the coffee shop, like, every other day," she explained. "And she would just order a coffee and sit there for hours."

Bess blinked, glancing from Maggie to me and back. "And?" she pressed.

Maggie looked at her blankly. "And that's it." She turned to me. "She was totally going there just to flirt with Jake. Everyone knows it."

"So let me get this straight," Bess responded, beginning to sound exasperated with her little sister. "Sarah had the nerve to go to a coffee shop, order coffee, and drink it? In front of a boy that Shannon was *not* dating? That's why Shannon tripped her in the cafeteria?"

Maggie frowned at Bess, then looked down at her hands. "She was going there to flirt with Jake," she replied insistently, her voice losing steam with every word. "Everyone knows it," she added in a whisper.

I glanced knowingly at Bess, then reached over and touched Maggie's hand. "Is Shannon nice to you?" I asked her.

"Of course she is," Maggie replied, not looking up. "Shannon is, like, one of my best friends."

Bess scoffed. "And what do you get to do as Shannon's best friend?" she asked. "Carry her backpack? Deliver nasty notes?"

Maggie glanced up and glared at her sister. "You just don't get it," she retorted.

I touched Maggie's hand again. "Maggie," I coaxed, "have there been any other incidents like the one with Sarah in the cafeteria? Any other girls who flirted with Jake, or did something else to upset Shannon?"

Maggie swallowed and looked back at her hands, hesitating.

"I'm not asking to get Shannon in trouble," I clarified. "I'm asking so I can have all the information and solve her case faster. No matter what Shannon did, nobody deserves to be harassed like she's being harassed now."

Maggie met my eyes then, considering my words, and sighed. "There was this one other girl," she replied. "I'm not sure why she and Shannon don't get along, but they don't. Anyway, she has this cow-patterned backpack, and in an assembly one day she went up to receive an award, and Shannon got everybody to start mooing at her."

Bess looked disgusted. "Is she overweight?" she asked.

Maggie shook her head. "No, she's actually really tiny," she replied. "It's just that she likes cows. And I guess Shannon thought it would be funny."

"What's this girl's name?" I asked.

"Gloria Suarez," Maggie replied. "She lives right on our block."

I got the address from Maggie, thanked her for her honesty, and stood up to go.

"You and I have to talk," Bess told her sister.

Maggie cringed. "I thought there were no wrong answers!" she cried. "I thought I couldn't get in trouble for this."

"You're not *in trouble*," Bess assured, standing up and squeezing Maggie's shoulder. "I think we just need to have a talk about what makes a friend, a friend." She glanced at me, and smiled. "Good luck, Nance."

"Thanks," I replied. "And really, thanks for your honesty, Maggie. I think this will be helpful."

Gloria Suarez's house was just three doors down from Bess's, a tidy ranch-style home with a rose garden outside and black-painted shutters. When I rang the doorbell, a petite, long-haired woman answered the door.

"Yes, this is the Suarez household," she confirmed. "You'd like to talk with Gloria? What is this about?"

"Actually, I'm trying to get to the bottom of a bullying incident at school," I explained. "I thought Gloria might be able to answer a few questions."

Mrs. Suarez looked horrified. "Gloria would never bully anyone," she insisted. "She's a quiet, good-natured girl. She keeps to herself."

I shook my head. "I don't think she's the bully," I clarified. "I just thought she might be able to answer questions about an incident she witnessed."

Mrs. Suarez looked thoughtful. "Okay," she said finally. "I'll take you to her room. But just for a few minutes."

I smiled. "Thank you. It shouldn't take much longer than that."

We walked down a short hallway, and Mrs. Suarez knocked on a door covered with soft-pencil drawings of animals and cartoons cut out from the Sunday paper. "Gloria?" she asked. "Someone is here to see you."

After a few seconds the door swung open, and I looked down at a tiny figure with long, black hair. Gloria was a good six inches shorter than I was, and her tiny frame was swallowed up by a huge T-shirt that showed a cow wearing a Statue of Liberty crown, with the words MOO YORK CITY stamped below it. She glanced up at me with confusion.

"I'm Nancy Drew," I greeted her. "Can I bend your ear for a few minutes?"

Gloria nodded mutely.

"I'll leave you alone," Mrs. Suarez said. "Gloria, let me know if you need me." She walked back down the hall to the living room.

Gloria looked up at me. "Um, come in," she said with a voice so soft I had to strain to hear it. It was like a dairy farm had exploded inside her room. Cow figurines, cow photos, stuffed cows, and cow-themed bedding all competed for attention. An actual cow-patterned *computer* sat on a small red desk—the only non-cow item in the room.

"Listen," I explained, "I don't want to take up too much of your time. I just wanted to ask you about a specific incident I heard about from one of your classmates."

Gloria looked at me skeptically. "Okay," she agreed.

"I've heard from a few sources that Shannon Fitzgerald can be a little mean sometimes," I said. "And I heard about one specific incident that involves you. I guess there was an assembly—"

Gloria's face paled, and she looked away.

"—an assembly where you had to go up to get an award," I went on. "And Shannon thought it would be funny if she got everyone to moo at you. Did that really happen?"

Gloria swallowed and shrugged. "Who'd you hear that from?"

I tried to meet her eye. Finally she looked at me, and I attempted to look trustworthy. "A reliable source," I replied. "See, I don't give away my sources. If you tell me what really happened, I won't tell anyone."

Gloria looked at me, seeming to consider this. She still looked so uncomfortable. "It happened," she said, in a voice just above a whisper. "But it was no big deal," she added, her voice rising as she looked away. "Shannon messes with everyone.

I'm sure she was just trying to make a joke."

I kept staring at her, trying to make eye contact again, but she turned away and started fiddling with a cow doll on her bed.

Shannon must cut a pretty scary figure at school, I thought. Nobody's willing to cross her.

"Okay," I said agreeably, hiking my purse strap up on my shoulder, as though I was getting ready to leave. "Just one more question: Do you know of a game called BetterLife?"

Gloria met my eyes then, just briefly, then turned and looked away. "What's it called?" she asked vaguely.

"BetterLife," I replied. And you know what it's called, I continued in my head. She was definitely familiar with the game. I could tell by the way she'd looked at me; I'd caught her off guard.

She shook her head. "I dunno, I think I've heard the name before," she said.

"It's a virtual-reality game," I explained to her, playing along. "You create a character, then live a whole virtual life online. I just created a character myself, actually. But you don't play?"

She shrugged. When I kept watching her, she shook her head. "No, I don't play."

You're lying. I took a deep breath. "Okay, then. Well—"

"Gloria?" Suddenly Mrs. Suarez appeared at Gloria's bedroom door, looking awkward. "I'm sorry, I didn't mean to interrupt. It's just that Gloria's friend is here to play."

Gloria glared at her mother. "*Mom*, we don't *play* anymore."

Mrs. Suarez smiled sheepishly. "Right, I'm sorry, *mija*."

I winked at Mrs. Suarez. "I was just leaving," I explained. "Thank you, Gloria, for answering my questions."

Gloria just stared at me. It took a steely look from her mother for her to reply, "You're welcome."

Hiking up my purse strap again, I followed Mrs. Suarez back down the hallway and to the front door. A young girl was waiting in the living room, staring at a game show on the television.

She glanced up as Mrs. Suarez and I passed, and I gasped at the same time she did.

Gloria's friend was Sarah O'Malley.

CONFESSIONS

I climbed into my car with a sigh, shaking my head. Sarah O'Malley and Gloria Suarez—two girls who were publicly humiliated by Shannon Fitzgerald—were friends. What were the chances? And what were the chances that these two friends had commiserated over their embarrassment, and decided to get revenge on Shannon?

I suddenly flashed back to my first experience on BetterLife, when Jake had shown me his character in the coffee shop. When I'd logged on as Shannon to show him what was happening to her, *two* bullies had been messaging her, wanting to know why she'd come to school that day. One was the girl I believed to be Sarah, with the

Celtic knot. And the other . . . Hadn't she had a pet cow?

Knock, knock, knock. I was startled as someone knocked on my driver's-side window, inches from my ear. When I finally calmed down and looked out, I saw Sarah and Gloria gesturing for my attention.

Wary, I lowered the window. "Yes?" I asked.

Sarah glanced at Gloria, and then looked to me hesitantly. Neither one of them seemed eager to continue the conversation. Finally, Sarah, fiddling nervously with an iPod clipped to her belt, announced bluntly, "We did it."

"You did?" I cried, the meaning of what she was saying almost overwhelming me. Was it possible that after all my questioning and noodling around in BetterLife, the culprits would just drop themselves into my lap?

Gloria nodded. "We bullied Shannon," she confirmed. "Some of the stuff you saw online— that was us."

"So which one of you is GuitarLvr15?" I asked.

Sarah looked concerned. "*Neither* of us," she admitted. "That's why we wanted to tell you. Gloria and I participated in the bullying, but we didn't start it."

I frowned. "Okay. Then who did?"

Gloria squirmed. "GuitarLvr15 did," she replied.

I sighed. This was getting frustrating. "And he is . . . ?" I prompted.

Sarah and Gloria exchanged shrugs. "We don't know," Sarah told me. "We only interact with him online. We don't really know anything about him, except that he hates Shannon."

"Wait a minute, wait a minute." I tried to make sense of all this. "How did you get involved in the bullying, then? How did you even find out this was going on?"

"He e-mailed us," Sarah replied, nervously pulling the plug for her headphones in and out of her iPod, over and over. "The day Shannon tripped me in the cafeteria, I got this e-mail from guitarzrcool@fastmail.net," she said.

I nodded. "That's the address Shannon got the first nasty e-mail from, and a few since then."

Sarah went on. "The e-mail said Shannon had been mean to too many people for too long, and it was time for her to taste some of her own medicine."

I nodded. "And?"

Gloria cleared her throat, speaking up. "A few days later, when she had everybody moo at me, I got the same e-mail," she said.

I furrowed my brow. I still felt like I was missing

something. "What did it tell you to *do*?" I asked. "If you were tired of getting bullied by Shannon, what action were you supposed to take?"

Sarah and Gloria exchanged glances. "It just told us to keep an eye on uVid," Sarah explained, "to look for videos with Shannon's character, Sassygirl48. It said they would give us the idea."

My mind was whirring. GuitarLvr15 wasn't only bullying Shannon, he was recruiting an army to help. "And what did you see on the videos?"

Gloria shrugged. "Sassygirl48 getting yelled at by random strangers. Sassygirl48 getting fired. Sassygirl48 having her house spray painted, and getting nasty letters."

Sarah nodded. "After a few days of watching those videos, we both got another e-mail from guitarzrcool. 'You can join in any time,' it said."

"Join in the bullying, is what he meant," I clarified.

"Right," agreed Sarah.

"And did you?" I asked, giving them both hard looks.

They both looked uncomfortable.

"I did," admitted Gloria. "You have to understand, I'm not a mean person. I've never bullied anyone in real life."

"But online's different," I supplied, not doing

a very good job of hiding my disappointment in these girls.

"Not just that," Sarah broke in. "You have to know how nasty Shannon can be. It's like you're not even a *person*, like you're lower than a speck of dirt on a worm. That's what she makes me feel like."

"Me too," Gloria agreed.

"I just—I didn't mean for things to go as far as they did," Sarah explained. "I never thought it would get this big. I just wanted her to experience being the bullied one, for once. I wanted to make her feel like she makes me feel."

I looked at Gloria. She nodded, ashamed. "Yeah," she said sheepishly. "Me too."

I sighed. It was like a nasty bullying cycle—from Shannon to these girls, then back to Shannon. No one felt any better for their nastiness; everyone felt worse.

"What about the others?" I asked. "Clearly you're not the only two helping GuitarLvr15. So are all of the other BetterLifers victims of Shannon, too? Trying to get revenge?"

Sarah swallowed. "Some of them are. I mean, she's been mean to a lot of people," she replied.

I nodded. "Okay. That's some. What about the rest?"

"I don't even know if they know Shannon," Gloria admitted. "I think some people—some people just saw the videos on uVid, and thought it was a cool thing to do."

Yuck. "Bullying Shannon was *cool*?" I asked.

Sarah shrugged. "Not cool," she replied. "Well, maybe . . . sort of. But more like it was this thing everyone was doing and getting excited about. I think people even tried to one-up one another—doing meaner, more outrageous things."

Gloria nodded. "And then people started being mean to her at school," she said softly.

"And Shannon got so upset she stayed home a few days."

Sarah winced. "Look," she said. "I know what we did was wrong. We're not proud of ourselves."

"You can say that again," I started to reply, then stopped myself, not wanting to sound like their mothers. "Listen, girls. This is very important. I want you to *promise* me that you'll lay off Shannon. No more bullying—in real life, in BetterLife, anywhere."

Sarah and Gloria nodded, looking at the ground. "We promise," they chorused.

"It doesn't make anyone feel better," I went on. "Does it?"

They glanced at each other. "No," Gloria admitted. "I kind of feel worse. I didn't want to freak out Shannon as much as we did."

I nodded. "Good. And to the extent that you can, I want you to encourage the others to stop."

"Okay," they agreed.

I sighed again, putting my keys in the ignition. "I want to thank you both for being truthful with me. If that's it, though, I'm going to go."

Sarah nodded. "What will you do now? About GuitarLvr15?" she asked.

I glanced from one ashamed-looking girl to the other. "I wish I knew," I replied honestly.

"Oh. My. God," Shannon greeted me a few minutes later. We were in her bedroom, and I had just shown up for our scheduled afternoon appointment. "Nancy, what has been going on? Do you have any idea what a nightmare school is for me? Did you know that someone drew all over the back of my new jacket with permanent marker, and people throw *food* at me in the cafeteria?"

"I didn't know that," I admitted. "Look, Shannon, I'm really sorry. No one should have to be treated like that."

Shannon's eyes filled with tears. "They broke

into my house in the game, Nancy. I can't even log on anymore; it's so upsetting. And at school, everyone except Rebecca just stares at me and laughs. When are you going to solve this, so the right people can be punished?"

I took a deep breath. "Listen," I began. "I'm working very hard to solve your case. And the good news is, today I learned who a few of the bullies are, and I think that may lead me to GuitarLvr15."

Shannon's eyes widened. "You know who some of the bullies are?" she asked eagerly. "Who?"

Uh-oh. I knew I was working for Shannon, but still, it seemed like the wrong call to tell her about Sarah and Gloria. She'd targeted them for humiliation before, and even if she wasn't as bad as I'd heard—even if Jake, Gloria, and Sarah had all been exaggerating—I would feel terrible if she tried to retaliate against them. Settling down on the edge of Shannon's bed, I tried to change the subject.

"Shannon," I said gently, "would you say you have a temper? Have you ever, say, said anything to a classmate that, thinking about it later, you thought was a little harsh?"

Shannon frowned. She seemed to have no idea where this line of questioning was coming from, and I couldn't blame her. "Uh, *no*," she replied. "I'm really nice at school. To everyone."

I nodded. "Do you know Gloria Suarez?" I asked.

A suspicious look passed over Shannon's face. "Sure," she replied. "We've been in school together since River Heights Elementary. Of course I know her."

I nodded. "The thing is, Shannon . . . I've heard from a few sources that there was an incident at a recent assembly."

Shannon's eyes suddenly seemed to burn with anger, but she quickly gained her composure. "Look, Gloria and I go way back. We're *friends*, okay? And friends rib each other sometimes. I know Gloria likes cows, so when she won the academic award at that assembly, I thought it would be funny if I mooed instead of clapped. When I did it, a bunch of other people joined in."

"It was a joke?" I asked warily.

"Yeah," Shannon replied, a defensive edge to her voice.

I swallowed, choosing my next words carefully. "Sometimes," I began, "we might think we're only joking with someone, but they don't think it's very funny. They feel hurt by it. Do you think that might be the case with Gloria?"

Shannon narrowed her eyes. "This is just like that Sarah thing," she complained. "Did you talk to her? Did you get that straightened out?"

I nodded. "I did talk to Sarah."

"And what did she say?"

"She said she tripped herself," I said truthfully, watching Shannon carefully. She looked triumphant, like this somehow proved her innocent on all counts. "But I think someone may have been telling her to say that."

Shannon glared at me. "Why would you think that?"

I sighed. "Shannon," I said. "I've heard from a few people that you can be a little tough on your classmates. I'm not trying to make you feel bad or tell you that you're a bad person. No matter what, no one deserves to be treated like you're being treated now."

Shannon's lip quivered. "But I . . . But I don't . . ."

I inched closer to her, placing my hand on her shoulder. "You don't what?" I asked.

Shannon's face began to crumple. "I'm not a bully!" she whined, then let out a strangled sob. "I can't believe you're accusing me! I asked you to help me because I'm being harassed, and you're trying to say *I'm* the bad guy!"

"Oh Shannon." I sighed again, rubbing her shoulder as she sobbed. "I'm not trying to say that. I just need the truth. What if you *were* mean to someone, and that someone knows something about what's happening to you now?"

Shannon sobbed. "The only person who knows who's behind this is—is GuitarLvr15," she insisted, shoulders shaking. "Do you know who he is yet?"

I shook my head sadly. "Not yet," I confessed.

Shannon stopped crying for a moment, and her eyes widened. "Do you know anything about him?"

I tried to smile. "I . . . Well, uh . . ." No? I racked my brain, trying to think of any identifying information we'd come up with. He liked to talk to people online? And not give away his identity? He drank virtual smoothies? "He . . . oh! He's really into music!" I said hopefully. "And he deejays sometimes."

Shannon looked at me blankly. "Really into *music*?" she asked disgustedly. "That's, like, everyone in my whole *school*," she scoffed. "Or anyone with an iPod."

Well, that burst my bubble. I shrugged. "I'm sorry, Shannon. That's all I have so far. But I told you when we first met that I would find who was doing this to you, and I intend to do that. I keep my promises."

Shannon blinked, wiping her eyes on her sleeve. "You'd better," she replied softly. "I don't know how much more of this I can take."

SECRET CRUSHES

Sarah O'Malley and Gloria Suarez, I thought, climbing back into my car. Both friends, both victims of Shannon's bullying. I started up my Prius and pulled out of Shannon's driveway. Both upset Shannon in some way, I thought. Gloria probably made Shannon jealous by winning her award . . . Sarah, by talking to Jake.

I stopped at a stoplight, thinking this over. Jake. Maggie had told us that Sarah had "stolen" Shannon's "boyfriend," but it had turned out, all she had done was talk to Jake at the coffee shop. If Shannon was so paranoid that Sarah just talking to Jake set her off, then surely Sarah couldn't be the only girl who had done that. Right? And maybe another girl who talked to Jake would also have been targeted by Shannon for bullying . . .

. . . and might be involved in the cyberbullying of Shannon.

When the light turned green, I made an abrupt U-turn. It was already getting dark, but I had something important to do downtown.

I had a few more questions for Jake Seltzer.

"Nancy! Fancy meeting you here!" A familiar, lightly accented voice greeted me as I walked into Barbara's Beans. I turned to the right, and spotted Ibrahim and Arij sitting at two computer terminals in the corner. They were both smiling, and judging from what was up on their screens, it appeared that they were both engrossed in games of BetterLife.

"Ibrahim, Arij!" I greeted them cheerfully. "How are you guys? How's school?"

Arij spoke up. "Very good, Nancy," she replied. "I've made some new friends, and we eat lunch together every day."

I nodded. "Good, good. Ibrahim, how's Better-Ibrahim4 doing?"

Ibrahim grinned. "Oh, very well, in the game," he replied. "He's gotten a good job at the Better-

Life bank, and I've enrolled him in night school, to get his degree in finance." He lowered his voice. "But unfortunately our friend from the other night has not spoken to him again."

I shrugged. "I guess that's not a surprise."

Ibrahim sighed. "I'm sorry I couldn't be more help, Nancy."

I gently touched his arm. "Don't worry about it," I assured him. "I appreciate what you did. Now if you'll excuse me, I need to speak with someone here."

"Of course, of course," he replied. "Do your thing. But if you have time, say good-bye on your way out."

"Sure."

Ibrahim turned back to his game, and I headed over to the counter. The shop was unusually quiet this evening, and Jake was leaning against the counter, staring into a television mounted on the far wall that was tuned in to MTV.

"Excuse me? Jake?" I asked.

He looked up. "Oh, hey there," he said in a friendly tone. "You again. Need some more BetterLife tips?"

I shook my head. "Actually," I replied, "I wondered if I could ask you some non-BetterLife-related questions."

He smiled. "Shoot. Ask me anything. My life is an open book."

"Well," I said confidentially, "listen. You're a good-looking guy, and you probably have girls coming in here just to talk to you a lot."

Two spots of bright pink appeared on his cheeks. "What? Come on. Whatever." He paused. "Did you ask me something?"

I tried to suppress my smile. "Um, I was really asking if any younger girls had come in here and hung out for a while, trying to talk to you," I explained. "Like, middle-school age. Girls coming in alone and chatting you up."

He looked thoughtful. "Not really," he admitted. "Oh, wait, there was this one girl. Dark hair, dark eyes? She looked about Shannon's age, actually. She used to come in almost every afternoon and order a decaf latte. She would sit right over there." He pointed to a table not far from the counter. "She would nurse that thing for hours. And yeah, she liked to talk. She especially liked to talk about music. Had mad cool taste for a younger girl."

I thought of Sarah—her long dark hair, and the iPod she'd been fiddling with incessantly when she and Gloria had told me they'd bullied Shannon. She took dance lessons, too. It stood to reason that she was into music. Just like Guitar-Lvr15. But that could be a coincidence. Hadn't Shannon said everyone in her class was into music? And Sarah had the ILoveDublin character. Why would she bother with that if she was already ringleading the charge against Shannon as GuitarLvr15?

In any case, Sarah had green eyes, not dark, but that was easy enough to miss. I pulled my attention back to Jake. "She had long hair?" I asked.

Jake nodded. "Yeah, long hair. She still comes in every once in a while, but she avoids me like the plague. She goes right to the computers and, if I'm behind the counter, she'll wait till I go off shift to order anything."

Ever since Shannon humiliated her into submission, I thought. So Maggie had been right about one thing: It seemed Sarah did have a thing for Jake. "Was there anyone else?" I asked hopefully. I so wanted him to say, *Yes, there was this other girl.* I wanted him to put me on the path of someone new. Someone who might be GuitarLvr15.

But he just shook his head. "Not that I can think of," he confessed. "I mean, someone might have come in once or twice. But I didn't notice."

"Right." It was almost completely dark outside. The colorful star-shape light fixtures in the shop filled the space with warm light. Suddenly a thought occurred to me. "Oh no," I muttered, looking at my watch. "Oh no! Thanks, Jake. I gotta go!"

I whirled around and ran for the door. It was 7:47, and my date with Ned was at eight. I barely had enough time to run a brush through my hair and book it to the restaurant. I was definitely going to be late no matter what I did. Fishing my cell phone out of my purse, I started dialing Ned's number to warn him.

"Nancy!" Ibrahim's cheerful voice drifted over from the computer terminal. He was sitting alone now. It looked like Arij had headed home. "Are you rushing home to check out the party at the virtual smoothie shop? GuitarLvr15 starts deejaying in about ten minutes."

The virtual party! "Oh shoot," I said out loud. My big chance to see GuitarLvr15 in a social setting—and hopefully gain some clues to his real-life identity. I'd completely forgotten.

"I . . . well, I . . ." I hesitated at the door. I knew I *should* check out the virtual party. I needed any info I could get on GuitarLvr15, especially after seeing Shannon today and how upset she was about the whole thing.

But . . . It had been so, *so* long since I'd spent

time alone with Ned. And what if I spent all night at the party and didn't learn anything new? Wouldn't I feel terrible for breaking my date?

"Shoot." I plopped myself down at the terminal next to Ibrahim and dialed Ned's number on my cell phone. It went straight to voicemail. He was probably on his way to Flavio's now.

"Ned, I'm so, *so* sorry," I said after the beep. "I don't think I can make it tonight."

PARTIES AND LIES

brahim looked at me curiously as I pressed the End button on my phone. "Did you have plans with Ned?" he asked.

"Yes," I replied with a sheepish smile. "I'm such a bonehead, I forgot about the virtual party on BetterLife. Thanks so much for reminding me, Ibrahim. I would have been kicking myself if I'd missed this."

Ibrahim beamed. "Don't mention it, Nancy," he replied. "I'm sure Ned will understand that your work on this case comes first."

I flashed back to the night of the lecture; Ned had seemed so upset that I'd wandered off and that we hadn't been able to spend any time alone together. "Yeah," I said slowly. "I'm sure he will."

I must not have sounded very convincing, because Ibrahim raised an eyebrow. "Do you think he will be upset?" he asked. "I know he cares for you, Nancy. I'm sure he must be disappointed not to see you. Who wouldn't be?"

I glanced up, startled by the sincerity in his voice. But when I caught his eye, he just smiled warmly. Ibrahim was such a sweet, friendly person. It was nice to have someone in my life who was so supportive and utterly upbeat. "Thanks," I replied, blushing a little. "I'm sure Ned will understand. I mean, he's such a good guy."

"Of course," Ibrahim replied, turning to his computer station. "Shall we get started? It's almost time for the party to start."

"Good idea." I turned to my screen and hastily logged on to BetterLife. When the familiar aerial view of the virtual River Heights came up, I took the mouse and guided it over to the—

"Wait!" I cried, grabbing Ibrahim's arm and pointing to the Username box.

It already had a name in it: GuitarLvr15.

"Whoa," Ibrahim said breathlessly. "The program remembers the last player who logged in from a certain computer. It's meant to make it easier for you to log in if you play at the same computer all the time."

My eyes widened. "So that means . . ."

". . . GuitarLvr15 was playing right on this computer!" Ibrahim and I chorused.

Wow. That meant that GuitarLvr15 was a customer at Barbara's Beans . . . or that he worked there. Suddenly I looked over to see who was working behind the counter: Jake was gone. A short-haired blond was now manning the espresso machine. Jake must have disappeared into the back. We hadn't seen him leave out the front door.

"Hmm," I murmured to myself. "I wonder if there are computers in the back."

"There are," Ibrahim responded, turning eagerly back to face me. "Once, when our father dropped us off here to do our homework, all of the computer terminals were busy, and the manager kindly allowed me to work in the back room until one became available," he explained. "There are two computers back there. They have all of the same programs as these computers, but they're older models."

I bit my lip. Hmm. I remembered the first time Jake had logged on to BetterLife to show me the game. It had been on this very computer! And then I thought of Jake's description of Sarah. The outgoing girl he'd described didn't sound like the reserved young lady *I'd* met. And he'd gotten her eye color wrong.

Which would make sense . . . if he'd been making the whole thing up.

"Ibrahim," I began, typing my username and password into the login box, "do you know if it's possible to have two BetterLife IDs at the same time?"

"Of course," Ibrahim responded. He had already been logged on to the game, so he was busy directing BetterIbrahim4 to the virtual mall. "I had several when I was first starting out. It took a few tries to get BetterIbrahim4 just right." He glanced up from the monitor, and smiled.

Nodding, I turned back to my own screen, where I picked up VirtualNancy at her apartment and got her moving to the smoothie shop, too. This was all interesting information. So Jake could be BionicEd . . . *and* GuitarLvr15. I glanced back at the counter. Jake was still missing.

But it was time to concentrate on the game . . . and the virtual party. BetterIbrahim4 and Virtual-Nancy arrived at the smoothie shop together. Sure enough, GuitarLvr15 was at the DJ booth. Every few minutes someone would go up to talk to him—making requests, maybe—but for the most part, he seemed lost in his own little world.

As a pretty redhead turned away from the DJ booth, I caught a glimpse of GuitarLvr15's T-shirt—and gasped.

"What is it, Nancy?" asked Ibrahim.

"His T-shirt," I replied. "It's a molecular diagram of caffeine."

Ibrahim glanced up at me from his screen, looking curious. "Oh. Does that mean something?"

"It could mean that he's into science," I replied, thinking of BionicEd. "And I happen to know that Jake has an interest in chemistry. Or at least, his other alter ego does."

Ibrahim looked confused. "Okay, but couldn't it also mean that he likes coffee? Caffeine? Get it?"

Oh. I sighed. If GuitarLvr15 was just a coffee fan, that *could* be Jake, who worked at Barbara's Beans, or it could be any of his customers. Probably many of Shannon's classmates among them. "Maybe," I replied. "Anyway, we'd better not try to talk to him. I don't want to make him mad. We can just blend into the background at this party, and observe him in his natural setting."

Ibrahim nodded. "Sounds like a plan."

So BetterIbrahim4 and VirtualNancy both got

strawberry smoothies—BetterIbrahim4's treat—
and settled on a couch to chat and keep an eye
on GuitarLvr15. A few strangers came up to us
and made conversation—nice kids, mostly, who
lost interest when they realized we didn't have
much of an opinion about the teachers at school
or the most recent sport in gym class. (I AM NEW!
Ibrahim explained, and a couple of kids took his
e-mail address to contact him in real life.) Mean-
while, GuitarLvr15 had a few visitors of his own.
As people approached him, I moved my mouse
over their avatars and clicked to view their user-
names.

"Butterflydust," I read. "Killerjoe4. Ibrahim,
these are all people who harassed Shannon in the
game!"

"I guess that's not surprising," Ibrahim replied.
"He is their leader, right?"

"Nancy?"

Suddenly a familiar, warm voice startled me
away from my computer screen. When I turned
around, there stood Ned: dressed to the nines in
a shirt and tie, holding a gorgeous bouquet of
pink roses. "Ned," I murmured breathlessly.

He looked at me with confusion, then looked
to my left. "Ibrahim? What are you doing here?
Where's Arij?"

Ibrahim shrugged. "She went home to begin her reading for her history class," he replied. "I stayed here, to surf the Net a little more."

Ned frowned. "How did she get home? I came to give her a ride."

"She walked," Ibrahim explained. "She said she wanted the exercise. And it's not far."

"I guess not," Ned agreed, looking down at the roses in his hand and then back to Ibrahim. "I thought you had a study group?"

"I did," Ibrahim replied. "It was canceled. The girl who was hosting it came down with the flu."

I looked from Ned to Ibrahim. I had been thrilled to see Ned, but strangely, he didn't look quite so happy. He looked . . . not quite annoyed, but . . . puzzled.

"I'm so sorry I had to break our date, Ned," I apologized. "It wasn't because I wasn't looking forward to it, believe me. It's just that something came up in the case."

Ned met my eye, a confused expression on his face, then looked behind me at the computer screen. "Is that BetterLife?" he asked.

"It is," I answered. "You know the case I'm working on has to do with BetterLife. I told you all about it before the lecture."

Ned swallowed. "I know, but . . . you broke our date to play a computer game?"

My mouth dropped open. I didn't know what to say. "Ned, you know——"

"Never mind," Ned interrupted me, holding up his hand in a my-bad gesture. "Never mind. I know you, Nance. I know that if you canceled, it must be something important." He paused. "I guess I'm just a little surprised to see you here." He glanced from me to Ibrahim. But Ibrahim had turned back to his computer and was directing BetterIbrahim4 to accept the invitation to dance from a curly-haired brunette.

I sighed. On my screen, VirtualNancy sat alone on the couch, sipping her virtual smoothie. Behind her, GuitarLvr15 sorted through a stack of CDs to pick the next tune. Was this really how I wanted to spend my Friday night? I wasn't learning anything new from the game. The one big thing I'd learned tonight was that GuitarLvr15 played from Barbara's Beans and that Jake mysteriously disappeared right around the time GuitarLvr15 was due to start deejaying. Maybe that was enough for one night. "Ned, you know . . . ," I began. "Maybe we should just go to dinner now. I don't know that I'm learning anything new from this virtual party, and——"

Suddenly I stopped. The song that GuitarLvr15 was playing. It seemed so familiar. Where had I heard it before?

And then it came to me. Dark hair, dark eyes. Loves music.

"Omigosh," I blurted, jumping up from my computer terminal and grabbing my purse. "I'm sorry, but—Ibrahim, Ned, I have to go!"

REAL-LIFE ANSWERS

"**W**hat are *you* doing here?" Rebecca greeted me as she opened the door to her bedroom. I'd called Maggie from my car, and she'd gotten me Rebecca's address from the middle-school directory. Rebecca's parents were out, and her older brother, who'd been absorbed in an extremely loud video game, had let me in without much more than a grunt. But Rebecca looked about as happy to see me as you might be to find a cockroach wandering out of your sandwich.

"We need to talk," I said, trying to walk past her into the bedroom.

Rebecca held out her arm to stop me. "I didn't

expect you," she whined. "My room is a mess! At least give me a chance to clean up before you come in."

I had a feeling I knew exactly what she didn't want me to see. I didn't want to be rude, but I *did* want to catch her in the act. "I don't have a lot of time," I insisted, pushing her arm out of the way. "We're all messy. I won't think any less of you." I barged in, Rebecca fluttering behind me, fidgeting and acting nervous.

"Can I—I mean, would you like, you know . . ."

Rebecca was doing her best to distract me, but there was no denying it: a laptop sat open on her desk, and on the screen was the profile for GuitarLvr15. He was still deejaying, but the song that was playing was coming to an end. Guitar-Lvr15 should have been cueing up another song, but he sat motionless. I glanced at Rebecca. She looked at me, seeming hopeful that I wouldn't catch what was going on.

The last notes of the song played, and we were plunged into silence.

I gestured to the computer. "You'd better pick another song," I advised. "Wouldn't want to let GuitarLvr15's many fans down!"

Rebecca's face fell. Caught! She sighed and, instead of walking over to the game, sat down on the bed and put her head in her hands.

"It was you the whole time, wasn't it?" I asked. "You created the character GuitarLvr15 to look like Jake, and get Shannon all excited when he started flirting with her. But all along you planned to humiliate her, and you made her humiliation worse by recruiting an army of cyberbullies."

Rebecca sighed, then looked up, trying to recover herself. "*Why* would I do that?" she asked. "Shannon is my best friend."

"She *was* your best friend," I corrected. "Until you both got a crush on the same guy. When Shannon found out you were hanging out at Barbara's Beans to flirt with Jake—the guy she thought belonged to *her*—she must have done something horrible to you," I mused. "Horrible enough that you didn't dare speak to him at all anymore. What is it that she did to you, Rebecca?"

She looked up at me, meeting my eyes. She looked miserable, like she knew she was caught. Finally she sighed again and said quietly, "She printed out all my personal e-mails."

I gave her a questioning look, and she went on, "E-mails that I'd been sending her all year. Not every single one—just the ones with juicy, embarrassing details. Crushes I'd had, stupid things I'd done, things I'd said about my other friends—things I never meant to go public." She paused. "She printed them all out and stapled them together into this packet. Later, she told me she was printing out *all* her e-mails, trying to make backups in case her computer crashed. But somehow this packet was only the worst of mine." She frowned at me. "She left it in our English classroom right before another sixth-grade class came in. So of course someone found it, and read it, and—" Her voice caught.

"And?" I prompted gently.

She gave me a rueful look, tears forming at the corners of her eyes. "It was all over the Internet by that afternoon."

Rebecca hastily wiped at her eyes while I absorbed this revelation. "And you're sure this was on purpose?" I asked.

She nodded. "Later, I told Shannon I thought it was strange that only *my* e-mails were in the packet, that only *my* e-mails had been left for everybody to see." She frowned again. "She told me maybe I should have stayed away from Jake. I asked why, and she told me she knew *I* knew what she was talking about. We never spoke of it again."

We were quiet for a moment. On Rebecca's computer, sounds of conversation got louder as virtual partygoers started filling in the silence left by the DJ.

"You never spoke of it again," I clarified, "but you hatched a plan to get revenge on her."

Rebecca nodded, staring down into her lap. "It wasn't supposed to go this far," she confessed. "It was just supposed to be me as Jake, making her feel stupid for thinking they could be together in the first place." She looked up at me. "I really meant it to be a few messages from me as him, and then over. She'd learn her lesson, and she'd never have to know it was me."

"But?" I asked.

"But," she continued. "One day I was careless. I was writing her an e-mail from Jake in the computer lab at school. Kind of mean stuff, about how she was so nasty to everyone else, now he was going to be nasty to her. And suddenly I hear a voice from behind me. 'What are you writing to Shannon?' It was Krista Mulgrew."

I nodded. "And who's she?"

"She's this other girl in our grade. Sweet but kind of dorky. She had a crush on this really popular guy, Doug, and Shannon found out about it and told him at lunch one day, right in front of her." Rebecca looked disgusted. "He made this big deal out of how he could *never* like her. Krista ran out of the cafeteria in tears." She paused. "I admitted to her what I was doing, trying to get back at Shannon. And she wanted to be a part of it."

I sighed. "And she had a BetterLife ID?"

Rebecca nodded. "She's Butterflydust."

I shook my head.

"It just grew from there," Rebecca explained. "I guess—I guess I was surprised to see that it really got through to Shannon. I've known her for years, and I've seen her do a lot of terrible things to a lot of people who'd done nothing to her. But it's like she's above it all. She can hurt you but you can't hurt her back." Her eyes flashed. "Well, I found a way to actually hurt her. I know it was wrong, but it felt *good*."

"Do you think Shannon deserved what you girls did to her?" I asked. "To be harassed every day at school, to lose everything—Do you think that was fair?"

"No," Rebecca admitted. "Shannon could be really nasty, but this . . . It went much farther than I meant it to." She paused. "To be honest, lately, I've felt bad about it. But there are so many other people involved now. . . ." She shrugged, looking ashamed. "I guess I just didn't know how to stop it."

"Well," I said, "we're going to figure out a way."

She glanced at the still-motionless GuitarLvr15 on her laptop's screen. I sighed again, going over all of this information in my head. Shannon had been a bully, and Rebecca had bullied her back. But when you added in the Internet factor to bullying, it got completely out of control.

"Can I ask you something?" I finally said.

"Sure," Rebecca agreed.

"If you didn't like the way Shannon treated people, including you," I began, "why not just stop being friends with her?"

Rebecca seemed to think that over. "I guess I wanted to keep my friends close but my enemies closer," she replied. "Besides," she added. "I like being popular."

ONE LAST LOG-ON . . .

The next morning I returned from a nearby meeting with Rebecca, Shannon, and their parents, feeling exhausted. After hearing Rebecca's story, I'd insisted on waiting with her for her parents to return from a movie, so she could tell them everything that had been going on. Naturally they had been horrified, and had set up a meeting the next morning between the two girls and both sets of parents.

"I can't believe it was you," Shannon had sobbed after Rebecca and her parents entered Shannon's kitchen. "You were my best friend! I trusted you!"

"But you were so mean to me!" Rebecca persisted. "You treat me like garbage sometimes,

Shannon. I wanted to show you what that felt like!"

After a long conversation and many tears from both of the girls, Shannon admitted that she sometimes wasn't so nice to her classmates.

"Why do you act that way, honey?" her mother demanded, looking completely shocked by all of these revelations. "What do you get out of being mean to people?"

Shannon's lip quivered as she glanced from her parents, to me, to Rebecca. "It—it—it keeps them from being mean to me first!" she cried, shaking her head and looking away.

"Why would they be mean to you?" asked her father. "You're a lovely, smart girl who's capable of being very sweet to her family and friends."

Shannon started to cry. "I don't believe that," she confessed.

It was a tough conversation, and in the end their parents decided that both Rebecca and Shannon should meet with a counselor for a while, to discuss why they felt they needed to bully each other. Mrs. Fitzgerald also volunteered to call the parents of the other kids involved and arrange a meeting at the school to discuss the rash of bullying at the middle school—and the advent of cyberbullying.

"I think a lot of kids will be grounded from the computer for the next few months," Mr. Fitzgerald predicted.

And that was just fine with me.

Now, I lounged on my bed and dialed up Ned. He answered on the first ring, which was a relief. I was afraid my call would go to voicemail, and I would be left to wonder whether he'd really missed it, or he was still upset about last night and avoiding me.

"Nancy? Is this my favorite detective?"

I smiled. "Ned, I'm so sorry about last night." I explained everything to him—finding Ibrahim at the coffee shop, the virtual party, how I'd realized Rebecca was behind the bullying, and everything that had happened since.

"Sounds like you've had quite an exciting twenty-four hours," Ned observed. "But let me ask about your *next* twelve hours. Dinner tonight?"

I grinned. "Yes, please."

We chatted for a few more minutes, catching up on everything we'd been doing the past few days and making concrete plans for tonight.

"Ned, I'm just so sorry for missing our date last night," I repeated, shaking my head. "You looked so nice, and the roses you brought were beautiful. I'm sorry for being so scatterbrained, and having to cancel."

"Don't worry about it," Ned reassured me. "I have another shirt and tie, and I've put those roses in water for you. We can just take up where we left off tonight, okay?"

I smiled, so relieved that Ned wasn't upset. "Okay."

There was a strange pause. "Just one thing, Nancy," Ned piped up suddenly.

"Sure," I replied. "What is it?"

"Maybe you shouldn't . . . spend so much time with Ibrahim," Ned said gently.

I was caught totally off guard. What? Was Ned jealous? Was he having second thoughts about having the al-Fulanis as houseguests?

"What do you mean?" I asked, but at that very moment Hannah called up the stairs.

"*Nancy!* Bess and George are here to see you."

Shoot. I'd invited Bess and George over to help me with the ceremonial laying to rest of Virtu-alNancy. Now that I knew who the cyberbullies were, I had no need for her.

"Nancy . . . ," Ned was saying.

"Never mind," I told him. "I'm sorry, Ned. We'll have to put a tack in this conversation. Bess and

George are here. Can we talk about this later?"

There was another funny little pause. "Sure," he said after a few seconds. "I'll call you later, okay?"

"Okay," I agreed, "thanks. We'll talk soon." I hung up the phone just as Bess and George appeared at my bedroom door.

"Hey, Nance. Are you *sure* you want to put Virtual-Nancy to rest?" Bess asked, pushing a sheaf of computer printouts into my arms. "I designed some cute new outfits for her that I'm sure would make her superpopular in the game, if you wanted to keep playing. There's a program you can download that lets you outfit your BetterLife character in your own designs!"

"And *Hack* magazine just published this new article about all the upgrades you'll get under the new subscription service!" George exclaimed, pushing a magazine at me. "It really sounds *incredible*. Are you sure you want to quit now?"

I glanced down at the printouts. Bess's outfits were gorgeous and chic. It looked like she had drawn them, and an amazingly accurate portrait of VirtualNancy, by hand. And George's article was filled with highlighted sections, with little arrows pointing to them and "Wow!" scrawled in the margins.

My friends were getting *way* too into this.

"I'm sure," I said, giving them both an apologetic smile. "Thanks for bringing this stuff over, guys. But I was really only on BetterLife to investigate my case. Now that it's solved, I think I'm done with so-called 'better lives.'"

Both Bess and George looked crushed.

"Okay," Bess murmured, reluctantly heading over to my computer.

"If you say so," George added, joining her.

The three of us settled in front of the screen, and I called up BetterLife and logged in.

WELCOME VIRTUALNANCY, the game greeted me. YOU HAVE $345, 4 FRIENDS, AND 22 MESSAGES.

"Twenty-two messages?" Bess asked. "That's kind of a lot, isn't it?"

George nodded. "The most we've ever gotten before was three," she confirmed.

"I guess VirtualNancy is getting more popular as she finds her way," I suggested, feeling a strange sense of pride. "Well, I'll just skim them." I clicked on Messages, then glanced down the list. At the top was an urgent one—from ILove-Dublin, or Sarah O'Malley.

"It couldn't hurt to see what Sarah has to say," I said, clicking on the message. We were here to end VirtualNancy's reign, but there was no need to be hasty.

Sarah's message contained no text, only a link to what looked liked a uVid video.

"Hmm," I muttered, clicking on the link. "Maybe something happened with the cyberbullies that she wants me to see."

The video began on a quiet residential street in downtown virtual River Heights. It soon focused in on a tall, dark-haired character. "That's Ibrahim!" I said happily. He was holding a letter and arguing with somebody.

"This seems unlike Ibrahim," I murmured. But then the game panned out, and I could see who he was arguing with.

I gasped.

It was VirtualNancy!

"This never happened!" I cried, turning to George. "I mean, I never played this part! How could there be a video of something I never made VirtualNancy do?"

George shrugged. "Just watch what happens," she advised. "Maybe you did this and forgot about it? That happens sometimes."

Captions of what each character was saying appeared on the bottom of the screen, like subtitles.

WHY WOULD YOU SEND THIS TO ME? Better-Ibrahim4 asked. I THOUGHT WE WERE FRIENDS!

VirtualNancy smirked. I WOULD NEVER BE FRIENDS WITH SOMEONE LIKE YOU, she replied.

"Omigosh," I whispered, glancing at George. "I *definitely* did not do this and forget about it."

George looked worried. "Then I mean—I guess the only other way is if someone hacked into your account and did this?"

PEOPLE LIKE YOU ARE RUINING THIS COUNTRY, VirtualNancy was telling BetterIbrahim4 now. WHY DON'T YOU AND YOUR FAMILY GO BACK TO IRAN?

Even in cyberspace, Ibrahim looked stunned. NANCY! he replied. HOW COULD YOU SAY THESE THINGS?

VirtualNancy turned away then, and pulled something out of her purse. I inhaled. It was a can of spray paint!

"Oh no," I whispered. "I'm not doing this, guys! What do I do? I would never do this!"

VirtualNancy walked away from BetterIbrahim4 and over to the apartment complex they stood in front of. Number 3C, a cozy-looking ground-floor apartment, had the name Better-Ibrahim4 posted on the mailbox.

VirtualNancy held up the can of spray paint and pushed the button at the top, releasing a stream of red paint onto the black front door.

Behind her, BetterIbrahim4 cried out in distress.

Bess, George, and I were stunned silent as VirtualNancy wrote her message on the door: GO HOME.

"Oh my gosh," I whispered, my chest aching with sympathy and shame. "Oh, poor Ibrahim. I can't believe this. I would never!"

The video ended.

"Wow," Bess muttered breathlessly.

Silently I closed the uVid window and returned to my message in-box. The page reloaded when I clicked back, and suddenly the number of messages changed: YOU HAVE 65 MESSAGES, the game told me. 17 OF THEM ARE URGENT. "People are probably watching this video right now," I cried. "They think I did that!"

I clicked on the first message. It was urgent, from MoomooGirl—Gloria Suarez.

THAT WAS RACIST AND DISGUSTING. I KNOW WHO U REALLY R, AND I'M LETTING PEOPLE KNOW. U SHOULD BE ACCOUNTABLE 4 UR ACTION.

My stomach fell. "Oh no."

My cell phone began ringing. I had a feeling I was going to have to turn it off soon. If even a tiny fraction of the people who played BetterLife in this town saw this video—and realized Virtual-Nancy was me—I could look forward to a lot of harassment in the next few weeks.

I clicked on the message below Gloria's, my heart squeezing when I saw the sender. It was from BetterIbrahim4, marked urgent.

The message consisted of only one word: WHY?

"I don't know, Ibrahim," I whispered, glancing over at Bess and George. They looked as angry as I felt. "But I'm going to find out!"

165